WILD IRISH SAGE

BOOK 10 IN THE MYSTIC COVE SERIES

TRICIA O'MALLEY

LOVEWRITE PUBLISHING

"I don't need to know everything. I just need to know where to find it when I need it."
– Albert Einstein

CHAPTER 1

*K*ira Delaney was interested in one thing
and one thing only – how to steal one of
the scones that had been delivered in a care package for
her mother, Aislinn. The basket brimmed with pastries, all
but taunting her from the counter of her mother's gallery,
and the lovely scent of cinnamon wafted her way as she
drifted closer. Still warm, Kira thought as she shot a glance
to the front window of the gallery. Gracie had already left
for the pub, so Kira should be in the clear.

She reached out, then paused as her phone buzzed on
the counter. Kira picked it up and rolled her eyes.

Don't you eat that scone.

I have no idea what you are talking about.

*Nice try. Take them to your mother. I magicked them so
if anyone else eats them without her permission, they'll get
sick.*

You wouldn't dare.

Okay, fine – try one.

"Damn it." Kira slammed the phone down and glared

at the basket of scones. In all likelihood, Gracie was lying. But did she want to chance that and risk spending the afternoon in the bathroom?

"Bloody magickal women. The power goes straight to their head."

"Excuse me?"

"Oh, I'm sorry – I didn't realize anyone was in here." Kira turned as she spoke, a shiver going down her neck, as she was someone who was typically quite aware of her surroundings. In more ways than one.

"I didn't mean to be startling you. I just wasn't sure if you were speaking to me." The man gave her a disarmingly sweet smile, his dark hair curling from beneath the knit cap he wore. Kira's senses stood at attention as his clear blue eyes met hers, and a lazy, languid warmth slid through her. Well, *hello*, she thought. The last thing she would have expected was to find a handsome man wandering a town where she knew everyone by name.

"I wasn't, at that. I was cursing my wily friend who has gone and dropped off some scones for my Mam and insisted that I can't have one for my own tasting."

"That's downright cruel, it is." The smile deepened in the handsome man's face and so did Kira's interest. Maybe there *would* be some enticing distractions to be found in little Grace's Cove over the next six months.

Kira's mother had recently torn a ligament in her knee and needed surgery. Unsure what to do with her gallery, Aislinn had asked if Kira would be interested in running it. Kira's photography career afforded her a flexible schedule so she had been happy to help, though she was certain her father had weaseled a few extra months from her so he could get a vacation out of it. He planned to whisk Aislinn away for an easy holiday in Portugal; she could paint by the beach during her recovery, and Baird could make sure she didn't overdo it.

It was Kira's first week reporting for duty, and already she was overwhelmed by how much was involved in running Aislinn's gallery. That must explain why she'd not even noticed there was a customer in the store – and a handsome one at that.

"It is. And I swear she can read minds. I was just about to sample one – just to be making sure they're tasty for Mam – and she messaged me to keep my paws off. You'd think she was spying on me." Kira leaned against the counter and shot the man a wide grin.

"Or perhaps just good instincts. It's hard to resist the smell, I'll admit."

"If you've a hankering for good scones, I suggest the café at the end of this street. They do a lovely pot of tea and clotted cream with the scones – you can't go wrong."

"I'll take that recommendation. The weather looks to be turning moody again, so I won't get further with any of my plans for the day."

"Traveling through, are you?"

"Not particularly." The man smiled at her, then turned to a rack of postcards featuring prints of her Mam's works. "I'll take a few of these and be on my way before the rain hits."

"Three for ten." Kira nodded at the rack and turned, her curiosity piqued. His aura – a rich blue with hints of green – suggested he was a man she would absolutely be interested in getting involved with. However, his non-answer to her question was slightly troubling.

Shrugging it off, Kira rounded the counter and stood by the cash register so the man could pay for his purchases before the clouds unloaded their burden.

"This is a nice gallery."

"Thank you. It's my Mam's. Aislinn is her name and she's the artist of these fine portraits you're buying postcards of." Kira tapped the postcards before sliding them into a small brown paper bag.

"Ah. I thought you might be the artist."

"I am an artist, but in a different medium." Kira smiled at him, leaving out any more information. After all, he hadn't been particularly forthcoming with his own details.

"I'm sure whatever you create must be equally as charming." The man glanced to the windows where the sky had grown darker. "That's me off, then. Now, you've got my mind on scones. A pot of tea will do just the trick. Have a nice afternoon."

"Same to you…" Kira let her voice trail off into a question, but the man didn't offer his name. Instead, he hunched into his raincoat as the first few drops splattered to the pavement.

She looked down at the banknote he'd given her. If she wanted, Kira could close her hand around it to see what insights it would give her on the man who had just held it. It was one of her gifts, passed down to her along with a few other more notable traits; it also tended to be one of the trickier tools at her disposal. Particularly where money was concerned. She'd not only pick up on the man who had just touched the money, but also several people before him. An item that passed through too many hands could give a very inaccurate reading.

"I hope he sticks around," Kira said out loud to the empty gallery as the skies opened up and rain tumbled down. She could do with a distraction or two, and a very delicious-looking man with a good aura would serve nicely.

"Sure and that girl is just trying to fatten me up now that I'm off my feet." Looking every inch a 'girl' herself, aside from the threads of grey that ran through her hair, Aislinn studied the basket Kira presented her with.

"True. Better not have any then." Kira turned, bringing the basket with her, and smiled when Aislinn let out a wistful sigh. "Just admit you want one, Mam."

"Well, I suppose I do want one. It's tremendously hard to say no to fresh-baked goods. But maybe you can share with me? That way, I won't eat them all."

"If I must, I must." Kira plopped down on a cushioned velvet chair in a deep mossy green color and handed her mother a scone from the basket, along with a little plate. The bedside lamp, its shade done up in stained glass, cast a rainbow of color across the navy-blue wall. Aislinn lived her life immersed in colors, and that had translated to her decorating style as well. Kira, having inherited some of her mother's traits, was also drawn to color, but she enjoyed the stark contrast of black and white for her portrait photography. The absence of color could sometimes be as startling as its presence.

"You must," Aislinn ordered with a smile, and Kira finally picked up her scone and took a bite.

"How's the knee?"

"You'd think I was an invalid," Aislinn hissed. "Not only did the surgery go well, but I had Gracie and Keelin up here doing their magick on me. I think my knee is stronger than it was when I was twenty."

"Likely so," Kira laughed, "but you know how everyone likes to fuss."

"I'm going out of my mind, I am," Aislinn said.

"Dad not letting you out yet?"

"I could run circles around the man. Where has he gotten off to now anyway?"

"Um, I think just to the shops," Kira lied easily, fully aware that Baird was likely having a pint at Gallagher's Pub.

"He's not to the shops. He's at the pub. And it's because I'm being a miserable twit, is why. I can barely stand myself, so I don't blame the man for sidling away for a nip of whiskey here and there."

"You're not used to taking it slow." Kira reached over and squeezed her mother's arm. "It's totally understandable."

"That's enough of me whining. Tell me how things are at the gallery."

"Today was slow, but that's just the weather and the time of year. Online orders are up thirty percent from last month."

"People are spending their Christmas money."

"That's my thoughts. Have you considered gift baskets for when tourist season starts?"

"Gift baskets? With art prints?"

"Well, you know, maybe more like a local artisan gift basket. You can add some of your jewelry, some pottery, some knitting – that kind of stuff. Not only would they get a beautiful piece of art, but also a few other pieces from around Grace's Cove. You could wrap it all nicely, maybe make little tags with a 'Grace's Cove Artisan' logo, something like that."

Aislinn had already grabbed a sketch pad from her bedside table, and her pencil dashed across the page.

"Something like this?"

Kira leaned over and peered at the image: an interlocking G and C, with a sprig of clover beneath it. "Perfect. It might be a way for someone to get all of their shopping done in one go."

"I like it. You're good for the business." Aislinn set the sketch pad down and studied her daughter.

Kira knew that look in her mother's eyes. "I'm not taking over the galleries for you."

"And why not? They're quite successful, you know." The gallery in Grace's Cove wasn't Aislinn's only shop; she had a few smaller galleries scattered around Ireland.

"I do know. Which is why Morgan kicks so much arse in running them, and running them well. I'm not a businesswoman, Mam."

"Well, now, that's a lie if I've ever heard one. You run a lovely business. Your services are in high demand. And you've got quite the social media following, not to mention a gorgeous website."

"Yes – as a one-woman show. It's too much hassle managing employees and multiple locations. I like my freedom of movement."

"What about just one location then?"

"Mam." Kira sighed. "You know I like to travel."

"So travel then. You can hire people to watch the gallery."

"Like you did?"

"Well, it's a bit different for me." Aislinn pushed herself further up the bed. "I'm the artist. Much of my time needed to be creating, which meant I had to be here. But you could still travel. You'd need to, anyway, to bring back more photographs to sell."

Kira had built a solid reputation in the world of photography, if she did say so herself. She'd covered everything from portraits of dignitaries and rock stars to animals in the wilds of Africa. It was tough for her to stick to one subject, and her propensity for moving between interests had actually strengthened her reputation as a versatile and flexible photographer. At this point, she was able to pick and choose her gigs, and she was always changing her plans based on her mood. It had led to a fluid and interesting life, and not one she was certain she was ready to change to man the helm at her mother's gallery in small-town Grace's Cove.

"I won't lie. It's always nice to come home," Kira admitted.

"See? You love it here."

"The people I love are here," Kira said. "That's a little different."

"I think if you gave Grace's Cove a chance as an adult, you'd be falling in love with it. Aren't you tired of living out of a suitcase? Don't you want someplace to settle, even if it is just a home base of sorts?"

"I'll admit, traveling does get tiring. There are moments where I wish for nothing more than the comforts of home. But!" Kira held up a finger. "I think those are also moments that I learn a lot about myself."

"You can learn about yourself here. Oh, Kira. Aren't you lonely?"

"That… well, the truth of it is… yes, at times my life is a bit lonely. Though I've made friends around the world." Kira didn't elaborate that 'friends' often meant lovers.

"I wasn't keen on that last *friend* of yours." Aislinn leveled a look at her daughter.

"Jax?" Kira kicked her feet out onto the bed and let out a dreamy sigh, mainly to cover the ache in her heart that still surfaced when she thought of him. Despite having worked with many a rock star in the past, she'd fallen for him – and fallen hard. She'd been certain she was different than the other groupies and that Jax had really cared for her. Perhaps he had, as much as he could care about anyone other than himself, but being an afterthought was not a role that Kira was interested in filling.

"Yes. The rock star who thinks so highly of himself." Aislinn sniffed, her disdain clear.

"He's good at his work."

"And a shite human to others."

"Ah, well," Kira said, "I suppose you've the right of it

there. I wish I'd seen it sooner, but I was mesmerized for a bit. Not as long as some of his other groupies, at least. But it pains me to admit how much I fell for him."

"That's a good thing, though."

Kira laughed at her mother. "How so?"

"I think we all need a bit of heartbreak in our lives. The sharpness of that loss defines our path forward. It clears the cobwebs from our vision, helping us to see what we want for our future."

"That's a nice way of looking at it. I think I'm a bit embarrassed as well. As a photographer, I'm meant to be objective, not to fall for my subject."

"Art is nothing without heart. You're being too hard on yourself. Because if it had worked out and he was the mad love of your life, then you'd be saying it was all meant to be. The point is…you gave it a go. And that's more important than anything. Never turn your back on a chance at love."

"You weren't saying that about Danny O'Sullivan."

"Ach, that lad was a mess and you and I both knew it." Aislinn tossed her curls over her shoulder. "A man who preferred a woman in her place and a pint in his hand. He'd never have made a good partner for you."

"No, I knew that too. But I enjoyed the flirtation."

"Thank goddess it never went any further than that."

"I never stayed around long enough. That's the point – my career doesn't leave me a lot of time for a relationship."

"I understand. But traveling like that must become tiring at some point. You've worked so hard for so many years… you've proven yourself as an artist. Over and over.

Isn't it time to take a break and see what staying in one spot would feel like for you?"

"Isn't that what I'm doing right now? I'll be here for months while you're gone."

"Sure and you choose to do this when I'm not around to spend the time with you," Aislinn grumbled, and took a bite of her scone.

"Well, don't go to Portugal then. I'll still stay here."

"Really? Hmmm…" Aislinn drifted away and Kira knew she was thinking about sunny beaches and delicious food.

"See? Take your holiday, Mam. You've earned it. How about this? I'll stay on for a bit longer once you're home so we get a proper amount of mother-daughter time."

"Promise?"

"Of course. You're right, I absolutely can take the time to slow down for a bit."

"You should explore around here more. Our wilds. We have some amazing spots for photography. You grew up wandering these hills. It might be nice to revisit them now that you've gained a new perspective."

"That's something I might just do. I do love our hills. Though… probably not today," Kira said with a laugh and a glance at the rain-lashed windows.

"No. Today is best spent on drawing. Let's figure out how the gift baskets could look. I need something to do with my energy."

"Of course." Kira bent to the notepad, and together they drifted the afternoon away.

CHAPTER 3

*S*he'd certainly left an impression.

Brogan McCarthy looked up from a recent study on land-use management and stared out the window at the pouring rain for the tenth time since he'd left the little gallery down the road. The woman at the shop had been right – not only did this café have excellent scones, but with a cheerful fire in the corner, lilting music in the background, and moody seascapes on the walls, it also provided a cozy haven from the rain. A variety of sitting spaces, with mismatched chairs and tables, made it feel like walking into someone's living room and being invited to stay for tea.

It was the perfect spot to settle in for the rest of the afternoon and go over some necessary paperwork, but Brogan couldn't bring himself to focus. And that was unusual, he thought, pushing the study back in its folder. Leaning back in the cozy armchair he'd chosen by the fire, he kicked his legs out and studied the rain falling in sheets outside the large front window. Periodically, a brave soul would wander past the window, head ducked and shoulders hunched, but for the most part, his view of the sea was unencumbered. The water was foreboding today, reflecting the stormy grey skies, and little white caps tipped the waves of the churning water. Fishing boats, moored for the day, were a burst of color in an otherwise morose picture.

Brogan loved it. He loved the sea as much as he did the land, and embraced nature in all its moody glory. If he didn't have paperwork to deal with, it was likely he'd be out in the rain, stomping through the hills and losing his thoughts to study the natural world.

But for now, his mind kept being drawn back to the lovely lass he'd met at the gallery. Too shy to ask for her name, he'd stumbled from the gallery feeling warmed from within – after only a few moments in her presence.

A lightning bolt, Brogan decided. That's what the woman was. When he'd turned and seen her at the counter, cursing at her phone, a flash of heat had struck him. A study in contrasts, the woman had worn leather pants with a wool sweater, her hair tumbling wildly about, with cool green eyes and warm red lips begging to be kissed.

Brogan shook his head and laughed at himself. Where had such a fanciful thought come from? As an environmental scientist, he wasn't much for flights of fancy. Instead, he stuck to studying the natural world, and he liked it when things made sense. This woman seemed like she would disrupt the natural order of things.

And yet…

He should've asked for her name, but he'd been too shy to make much more than basic polite conversation before he'd hustled himself out the door. Maybe one of these days, he'd wander back down to the gallery and see if he could talk her into having a drink with him. At that thought, Brogan outright laughed at himself. He was about as good at wooing women as he was at painting – both of which left a lot to be desired. It wasn't that he wasn't confident in who he was or what he wanted out of life – he was just a quiet sort. Brogan preferred roaming the hills and communing with nature to hitting the party scene. He'd learned, though, that women were naturally drawn to He Who Commanded The Most Attention – a title Brogan would happily leave to someone else.

"Having a laugh with your demons?"

Brogan looked up to see a man appraising him with smiling eyes and just enough scruff on his face to warrant calling it a beard.

"I suppose I am at that," Brogan admitted.

"This seat taken?" The man gestured to the armchair on the other side of the fire.

"All yours."

"Thanks. Nice day to hunker in."

"That it is. Though I'd prefer to be out in it," Brogan admitted. "I'm Brogan."

"Liam. You new to town? Or just traveling through?"

"A bit of both. I'll be staying here for a while until I figure a few things out. Then…" Brogan spread his hands wide in front of him. "We'll see."

"A man after me own heart. Though I'm much more settled these days. Careful, this town has a way of digging her hooks into you until you want to call it home."

"From what I can see, it's not such a bad place to live."

"Where's home for ye?" Liam smiled as the server

brought him an Irish coffee in a tall glass with thick cream at the top.

"Not too far down the way – Kinsale."

"That's a lovely spot, it is. Arguably as lovely as here, actually."

"It is. But when you've known it for much of your life, it's always good to explore. I've spent the last years in Dublin, though. I'm ready to be out of the city again."

"I like cities, I truly do. But only for a visit, that's the truth of it. I'm a man of the water, and prefer the small quarters of a ship over the confinement of a city. If that makes sense."

"Sure, because the boat is always moving and the ocean is vast."

"That's exactly it." Liam jabbed a finger in the air. "Cities feel like they close in around me."

"I'm much the same, I'll admit. It's the land I'm needing, not another shop."

"Exactly. So, Brogan, what's on your list to explore here?"

"Largely the land. But I'd also like to try a few restaurants in the village here, as well. My cooking will get old quickly."

"As you should. Well, welcome you are, then. We're a small village at that. You'll know everyone's name in a matter of weeks, I'm sure of it."

"Doubtful," Brogan laughed. "I have a tendency to keep to myself."

"By choice? Or habit?"

"A bit of both, I suppose." Brogan took a bite of his scone, letting the blueberry flavor settle on his tongue as he thought it over. "I don't need a lot of social interaction to be happy. I'm content with my work so long as I can get into nature."

"We all need friends, though."

"Of course. You're right, I think I just fall into a routine of keeping to myself, then realize I haven't bothered to socialize when I really should have taken the time to."

"Well, I'm happy to introduce you around. Even if you're here for work, it's always good to have a few lads to have a pint with on occasion. Come meet us at the pub sometime this week? You can meet the lads."

"I'm game. I'll need to make a few contacts here anyway." Brogan didn't elaborate and Liam didn't ask. Brogan immediately liked that about him – a man who kept his own counsel and wasn't too nosy. Not that he was doing anything that warranted hiding, but it was nice to know whom he could trust if he needed it down the road.

"Here's my card. Give me a call when you're ready for a pint. You'll find me at the pub many a night – they have good company and good food. I'm not always in a mood to cook and my fiancée, Fi, isn't particularly focused on whipping up a meal these days."

Brogan surprised himself by asking, "Is she pregnant?" Now who was being the nosy one?

"I hope not!" Liam threw his head back and laughed. "She's started a new job translating novels. I can barely make a noise in the house these days. I'm finishing up the conversion of a bedroom to her office and moving her into it this week. Right now, she's working at the dining table."

"Ah, yes. A dedicated workspace will make a difference."

"I just need to figure out a way to make her think it was her idea first."

"You're a smart man."

"I like to think so." Liam finished his coffee and stood. "Nice to meet you, Brogan. Hope to see you around."

"Same to you." Brogan was surprised to realize he meant it. That was two people in one day who'd left an impression on him. Maybe Grace's Cove would be exactly what he needed to pull himself out of his funk after all. Time would tell.

CHAPTER 4

"This one's in a mood," Gracie said, nodding at Kira, while Fi helped her cut lavender for one of her tinctures. The three of them were having a cozy girls' night at Grace's cottage on the cliffs, with Liam on tap to drive Fi and Kira home later that night. Kira had brought a pizza, and they'd already worked their way through one bottle of red wine.

"She is, isn't she? I was going to wait her out and let her tell us what's going on," Fi said.

"We'd be here all night. You know how she is."

"I guess," Fi agreed. "She's always been stubborn with her thoughts."

"Not like we can't see her mood hovering around her."

"I'm right here." Kira glared at the both of them and reached for another slice of pizza. "You do realize that you could include me in this conversation?"

"And why should we? It's not like you'd be bothering to tell your best friends in the world what you're stewing about." Grace leveled Kira a look that had her rolling her eyes.

"I'm not withholding anything. I don't know why I'm in a mood. I can't be really telling you what's going on if I can't pinpoint it myself, can I?" Kira took a bite of cheesy gloriousness and thanked the goddess that Grace's Cove had finally opened one minuscule pizza parlor.

"We could help," Fi suggested. "If you talk instead of brood, we could get to the bottom of it."

"Are you missing that rock star? What's his name – Baz? Racks?"

"Jax," Kira sighed. "And, no. I don't miss him."

"He hurt you." Gracie zeroed in on Kira's face.

"He did. But you know what the truth of it is? I think I really hurt myself."

"How so?" Fi asked, leaning across the table to pour more wine into Kira's glass.

Kira leaned back and closed her eyes, bringing Jax's face to mind while she tried to think of the best way to explain her complicated feelings about having dated him. It had been a relationship at high speed, full of dramatic swings and unrealistic moments, but she supposed that was the nature of dating someone famous.

"Honestly, I'm disappointed in myself. I thought I was smarter than the others. That I wouldn't fall under his spell. But… I did. Even when I could see the truth of him. Even when I knew he was only capable of caring about himself. For a moment, I thought – what if I was the one who could make him see or feel differently? I suppose that's me thinking a little too highly of myself." Kira gave a half laugh and pushed her tumble of curls over her shoulder.

"You fell in love with the future you hoped for, not the reality," Fi said.

"Exactly." Kira nodded and took another sip of her wine. "I guess every woman wants to be different or the special one, you know?"

"Of course. It's natural," Gracie said. "But from where I'm sitting – I'd say you're being much too hard on yourself."

"You think?"

"Yes!" both Fi and Gracie exclaimed.

"Well, then, tell me how you really feel," Kira grumbled. She bent to pet Rosie, Gracie's dog, who had come to rest her head on Kira's leg.

You should give me a piece of pepperoni.

"Is that right?" Kira looked down at Rosie and stroked her ears. "I'm not sure how your Mam will be feeling about that."

"What does she want now?"

She won't mind. She sneaks me pepperoni when nobody's around to see.

"Rosie's telling me all your secrets." Kira laughed at Gracie.

"What's she saying?"

"That you tell us not to feed her from the table and then sneak her pepperoni when nobody's around."

"Rosie!" Gracie put her hands on her hips. "That's a sure way to never get pepperoni again."

She doesn't mean it. She loves me.

"She says you love her and you'll still give her pepperoni."

"She's not wrong," Gracie laughed and pulled a pepperoni from a slice of pizza. "You're the best dog in the world, my sweet Rosie. Of course, you can have a piece of pepperoni."

Love you. Love you. Love you.

"She says she loves you," Kira said.

"I could get that much from her body language," Gracie laughed as a delighted Rosie wiggled her bum like crazy.

"Did you ever tell Jax about any of...?" Fi waved her hand in a circle over the table and Rosie.

"No, of course not. I mean, I don't really hide it from people I love but..."

"So you didn't really love him then," Fi said.

"I was certainly infatuated."

"It's not wrong to hope for more. I get where you're feeling a bit foolish to ignore the signs. But... maybe you can reframe it?" Gracie asked.

"How so?"

"Like instead of feeling like a fool for not reading the signs, maybe you can just be grateful for the experience? You certainly learned something from it. And you had some pretty cool experiences out of it. I mean, you got to meet Mick Jagger! How fun is that? Maybe once you stop being so critical of yourself, you can just enjoy it as a story you tell in your older days of having a lurid affair with a rock star back in your wild and misspent youth."

Kira felt the tight bands of angst in her chest start to ease. Gracie certainly had a point. If she was able to change her view of the relationship, maybe it wouldn't sting so much.

"You might have a point there, Gracie. I'll admit, I did get to experience some really cool things."

"See? He was just a fun tool to be used. Plus, you took some really amazing pictures," Fi said. "That one where the rain was coming down over the stage and a lightning bolt was in the background? Magick."

"They made that one the upcoming album cover," Kira said, then slapped her hand over her mouth. Technically, she'd just violated her non-disclosure agreement.

"Did they? That's amazing!" Fi leaned over and gave her one-armed hug. "Congrats to you!"

"Well done, Kira. I'm proud of you." Gracie nodded and added another ingredient to the silver bowl in front of her.

"Nobody's allowed to know that yet."

"Don't worry. Nothing leaves the sacred enclaves of girls' night," Fi promised.

"So, if Jax isn't what's got you in a mood – what does?"

"I can't really say." Kira shook her head and picked up her slice of pizza again. "It's like... I'm certainly happy to be home and see everyone. But I've been moving at such a fast pace for years, always taking the next assignment, that I'm not sure I really know how to stay in one place for long."

"It's an adjustment, that's for sure." Fi had, up until recently, traveled almost as much as Kira. She'd now settled back into Grace's Cove and had completely revamped her career. From where Kira sat, it suited Fi well.

"How are you finding it? Being here all the time, that is?" Kira ignored Gracie's snort. Gracie loved her cottage on the cliffs and her gorgeous husband, and would happily spend the rest of her days in Grace's Cove.

"I'm quite comfortable with it, I think because I know Liam and I have plans to travel. I'm enjoying my work and I like knowing I can leave when I want. It's nice to have a home base again. Traveling can get lonely."

"It can also be really exciting," Kira said.

"I think it's more exciting when you have a partner to go with you," Fi said, then shot a guilty look at Kira. "I'm sorry if that's sounding mean. It wasn't meant to hurt you."

"No, it doesn't. I'm certain you've the right of it. Traveling with a partner is probably much more exciting."

"Let's get her a date." Gracie perked up and shot Kira a wicked smile. "You need someone to distract you while you're here."

"Oh, please. You know how dating in this town is. Everyone will have their noses in my business in two seconds."

"And what's wrong with that? It can be fun to be the talk of the town."

"No, thank you." Kira glowered at her and buried her nose in her wine.

"Who should we set her up with?" Fi mused, completely overriding Kira's objections.

"I don't know. That's a bit of a problem, isn't it? Not much to pick from here." Gracie stopped what she was doing and leaned back, looking to the ceiling for answers.

"I do not need a date."

"What about Paddy?"

"He's ten years older than her," Fi laughed. "That's a no."

"Sean Connelly?"

"He's a crush on Mary Ellen."

"Ah, I hadn't heard that yet."

"This is what I'm talking about, Rosie," Kira grumbled to the dog, who had returned to put her head on Kira's leg again. "Everyone knows everyone's business."

Pizza.

"You're right. Pizza is the answer." Kira peeled off another slice of pepperoni to give to the dog.

"We need some time to think on this. I'm sure there has to be at least one option." Gracie smiled at Kira, a determined look in her eyes.

"I did meet someone the other day."

"Did ye now? This one here's keeping secrets from us." Gracie raised an eyebrow at Fi.

"As well I should. You two will have me married off before I even go on a first date."

"Not true. Her, maybe," Fi said, pointing to Gracie. "But I'm taking it slow with Liam. No wedding on the books yet."

"And why not? You know you're the ones for each other."

"Because we can do it on our own time, thank you very much. You are not Mistress of the Universe just because you're all-powerful, Grace."

"I should be. The world would run much more smoothly if they just let me handle everything."

"Like you have time for it," Fi said, and the two began to argue.

Kira smiled and shook her head. Stroking Rosie's soft ears, she thought about the man at the gallery the other day. He'd lingered in her mind long after he'd left, and she'd hoped to see him around town. There was something about his aura that had rung true to Kira, not to mention a smile that had warmed her to the core. She wished she'd gotten his name.

"She's daydreaming now, she is. This one goes from moody to lovesick in a heartbeat." Gracie snapped her fingers in front of Kira's face, jerking her out of her thoughts.

"Lovesick? Please. I barely know the man."

"See? She's withholding details. This must be important." Gracie glanced at their now-empty second bottle of wine, and moved from the table to the long shelves that lined the wall. Pulling a bottle of whiskey from the shelf, she motioned for Fi to bring the glasses. "We're on to the whiskey for this story."

"It's not a story that needs whiskey. It's not anything."

"Every story pairs well with a good Irish whiskey. You should know that." Gracie held up the bottle. Grace O'Malley Whiskey – a whiskey named after her own rebel pirate spirit, and one they'd been delighted to discover. It wasn't every day that the reincarnated soul of Grace O'Malley herself got to drink a whiskey named after her.

"I won't say no to that whiskey, seeing as it has your name on it, but really it's nothing." Kira held up her glass to the others. "Sláinte."

"Tell us anyway," Fi pressed.

"It was just a handsome guy in the gallery the other day. Good aura. He's lingered in my mind is all."

"What's his name?" Gracie asked.

"He didn't say. Just that he's in town for a bit, not just passing through. Really, I didn't get much from him. But I'd like to know more."

"We'll find him easily enough," Gracie promised. "A few phone calls is all it takes."

Kira laughed. "No, really. Don't start this. If it's meant to be, I'll run into him of my own accord."

"I wonder if that's the lad Liam met at the coffee shop?" Fi mused. "Said he'd run into someone new to town who seemed friendly. Asked him to come 'round for a pint and he'd introduce him to a few people. Brogan was his name, I believe."

"Was he at Ann's Café? Like two days ago during the storm?"

"Aye, that was it."

"That's the man, then." Kira shook her head at just how small the town really was.

"Brogan, huh? Now, why does that name seem familiar? I feel like Fiona was friends with a Brogan or something," Gracie said. "I'll ask her the next time she rudely pops in without invitation." The last bit was said loudly to the ceiling so that if Fiona was near, she'd hear it. Turning to Fi, she said, "And you let us know when Liam goes for a pint with this Brogan."

"No, please. I do not need you two meddling." Kira raised her glass and glared at the both of them.

"Who said anything about meddling? I just want to take a peek," Gracie said.

"I can't be getting in trouble if I accompany my man to the pub now, can I?" Fi said, her voice deceptively sweet.

"And this is why I don't live here anymore." Kira groaned and dropped her face into her palms.

"Don't worry. You'll get used to it again," Gracie promised.

"I hope not."

CHAPTER 5

*K*ira took to the hills.

It was what she always did when she needed to mull over her thoughts – she went for a wander. Preferably in nature, when her location allowed. Morgan was doing inventory and spreadsheets at the gallery today, so Kira had been all but shoved out the back door and given a free day.

Out of habit, she'd slung her Nikon around her neck, tucked a rain jacket in her side pack, and laced up a sturdy pair of waterproof boots.

Today the air was crisp, hints of spring coming to her on the wind. Kira turned her face to the sky where the sun struggled to peek out from behind the clouds. She loved the time between seasons, when things were changing and growing, or being put to rest. That in-between time – when nothing was certain – had always fascinated Kira. It was also why she liked taking photos of people at difficult moments in their lives. It was during times of transition that true character shone through.

She'd parked near Grace's cottage, waving to her through the kitchen window where Gracie had thrown the shutters open. Kira didn't bother her, knowing she had a big order to fulfill, but Gracie had nudged the door open so Rosie could join Kira on her wander. There was something nice about a friendship like this one, Kira mused, where she could show up on someone's land, yet each woman knew the other needed to be alone.

"It's still chilly, Rosie. You'll tell me if you need to go back, right?"

I like it.

"Okay then. Just run around more if you need to warm up."

Running is my favorite!

True to her word, Rosie raced in front of Kira, stopping to sniff different bushes and mark her territory.

Kira veered right, away from the cliffs; she was not in the mood for any messages from the cove today. Instead, she climbed higher into the hills behind Grace's cottage, picking up a walking stick along the way to help her over some of the more difficult areas. Rosie navigated the climb with ease, turning back periodically to check on Kira, but they kept their own counsel as they walked.

Kira paused as she rounded a turn, surprised to discover a small pond that looked to be fed by a trickle of a river running through larger cliff faces. It was partially shaded by higher cliff walls and open on the other side to the hills below that rolled all the way to the sea, and Kira was certain she'd just found her secret nirvana.

"Why have I never seen this spot before?" Kira said

out loud, turning in a full circle and automatically mentally framing up the photos she would take.

Takes time to walk here.

"It does, but it's certainly worth it, isn't it?" Kira smiled down at Rosie. "Mind if we stay a bit? I want to take some photos."

Stay! Stay!

"That settles that." Kira laughed. Picking up her camera, she fired off a few shots on instinct alone, knowing that often her first shots were her best ones. Walking around the curve of the pond, she found a few smooth boulders tucked together to form a natural seat, and pulled herself on top of them. Settling her back against the rock, Kira brought the camera to her eye.

Hair?

Kira turned to look at where a little goldfinch had landed on the rock next to her, tilting its head to study her.

"You want a strand of my hair for your nest?" Kira asked, watching as the bird hopped closer to look at her riot of curls, which she'd pulled loosely back in a band.

Hair?

"Sure, then. You can have some hair." Kira pulled the band from her hair and ran her hand through her curls until she had several tendrils. Winding them around each other until she had a thick little loop, she held it out to the goldfinch and waited.

The bird understood Kira's intention immediately, and hopped forward to pluck the hair from her hand before flitting away. Smiling, Kira leaned back against the rock to watch the natural world go about its business around her.

She couldn't have pinpointed when she'd figured out that she could speak with animals. There hadn't ever been one defining moment where she had realized it; it was just something she'd always known. It hadn't taken Aislinn long to figure it out, or so she would tell it, after she'd found toddler Kira babbling to the cat in the garden. After that, Aislinn had watched Kira and had come to realize that all the animals followed her closely. It was a gift that not many of the other women had, though Gracie was fairly good at understanding an animal's needs.

Not like Kira, however. Kira could hear their thoughts directly communicated into her brain. She'd had to work diligently at not revealing it when she traveled or was in a group of people. Not that Kira hid her abilities, exactly – but it was easier to point out that a dog looked hungry than to say that the dog had asked her directly for help.

More than one lover or friend had certainly freaked out when she'd revealed what her gift was. Kira chuckled at that. Unlike her cousins, she wasn't as concerned with hiding who or what she was. Granted, she didn't lead with the fact that she could see auras, talk to animals, and touch items to get more information from them. But it wasn't something she took great care to hide either.

One thing Kira had learned pretty quickly was that the people who accepted her magick would stick around, and those who viewed her as a freak would leave. It was an easy way to weed out the closed-minded.

A ripple in the water pulled her from her thoughts, and Kira tilted her head to zero in on the movement. It wasn't a fish, for the ripple continued across the surface. When a furry head popped up, Kira let out a laugh of delight. An otter! It had been ages since she'd seen one. Wondering if it would talk to her, Kira slid off the rock and approached slowly, not wanting to startle the little otter. Finding another rock on the shoreline, she settled herself by the water's edge and waited quietly while the otter gave her the side-eye.

"Friend," Kira said, both with her mind and her voice.

Friend?

"Friend," Kira confirmed.

The otter took its time, though she knew them to be curious animals, and paddled about before finally swimming closer.

"I'm going to take your picture," Kira said, again with her mind and her voice. She knew that animals understood her intent when she spoke with them, but she wasn't sure if it was because of her thoughts or her voice, so she always communicated both ways. The otter didn't say anything back, but he also didn't swim away. Kira took that as permission and put her camera to her eye. She smiled as the otter did a series of little twists and turns, tilting his head to the camera, almost as if he was on a little photoshoot.

"You are absolutely darling."

Help.

"What? You need help? What's wrong?" Instantly on her feet, Kira looked around to see what could be wrong.

Our water is going. It used to flow big. Now very small.

"Your water? You mean the stream?"

Kira turned to walk to where the pond was being fed by the small stream through the hills. Once she was closer, she realized that the small stones and pebbles around the water were indicative of what had once been a much wider river. Now, only a small stream, about two feet wide, ran down the middle of it to feed the pond. Looking at the area with new eyes, Kira could see where the edges of the pond must once have reached much further.

Returning to where the otter now sat on the side of the pond, shaking his fur off, Kira crouched to meet his eyes.

"What's happened?"

Builders. Big machines. Noise. Shite.

"Did you just swear?"

Shite.

"Where did you learn that?"

Men.

"It must be developers," Kira said, turning again to look. From where she stood, she couldn't see any construction.

Yes.

"Have they cut off your stream?"

Yes. Much smaller.

"I'm sorry. I don't know anything about this. But I'll find out for you. I'll help."

You help.

"I'll help. I promise. I need more information."

The otter seemed satisfied with that, and an idea sprang to her mind.

"A few more pictures."

Yes.

Kira busied herself taking several more portrait photos of the otter, laughing as he played it up for the camera. He really was darling. She'd have to name him, Kira thought, already building her idea in her head.

"Do you have a name?"

Name.

"Do you have one?"

Name.

"Okay, I'm guessing that's a no. Can I give you one? So I know it is you?"

Yes.

Oh shoot, Kira thought, her mind scrambling to come up with a name that wouldn't insult the otter. The fact that she was sitting there trying not to hurt an otter's feelings was something she'd examine another time.

"How about Fergal – meaning brave. Does that suit?"

Yes.

"Fergal, I'm going to look into this for you. I'll try to be back soon and see what can be done."

Others need help. Not just my family.

"I hear you. I promise I hear you. I'll see what I can do."

Blessed be.

Interesting that an otter understood the natural blessing, Kira thought as she waved goodbye and whistled for Rosie. She'd come on this walk to mull over thoughts of what she was doing with her life at the moment, and now she was heading back home thinking about otters.

Despite how much she loved nature, Kira had to admit she knew very little about otters, other than that they were very cute and she saw them rarely. If she truly wanted to help Fergal as she'd promised, then she needed to spend a little time researching what they needed in a habitat.

But first, Kira decided, she needed to set up a new Instagram account – one dedicated to the otters of Ireland and their actual personalities. One thing she'd learned over the years was that people responded best to animals when they could humanize them.

It was time to make Fergal famous.

CHAPTER 6

*K*ira rolled over and pulled the pillow over her head, ignoring the persistent buzzing that came from the bedside table. She'd stayed up much later than she'd planned to last night, lost in researching otter habitats and building up an otter-themed Instagram. After she'd edited her photos and chosen a user name – In Otter News – she had posted a particularly fetching photo of Fergal looking warmly at the camera. She'd captioned it, 'We need each otter.'

Pleased with her work, she'd added a brief line about otter conservation and then went to bed, determined to look more deeply into the developers the next day.

She had a moment or two wondering if this was really worth her time, but Kira reminded herself that not all of her assignments were fancy paid gigs for rock stars or magazines. It wasn't uncommon for photographers to take on a charitable gig here and there, and Kira didn't see any reason why an environmental conservation project couldn't be hers. Not only was it a noble cause, but the otters were seriously cute. She couldn't deny they needed help, and if it gave her a purpose while she was in Grace's Cove, then so be it. Win-win, as far as she was concerned.

"I didn't set my alarm so early, now did I?" Kira grumbled, pushing her mop of hair out of her face and closing one eye to squint warily at the phone. Seven in the morning! She wasn't due at the gallery until at least nine. Sighing, Kira swiped open her phone to see what the notifications were about and then sat straight up in bed.

"Well, sure that was fast, wasn't it?" Kira looked out the window toward the water and wondered if Fiona, Gracie's departed great-grandmother and resident ghost, had used her powers from the other side to give Kira's Instagram account a push. Kira let out a delighted laugh when she saw her follower count had reached just under five thousand people in one night. Knowing it was best to capitalize on any momentum – an object in motion and all that – she found a cheeky photo of Fergal. Pausing for a moment, she mulled over captions before typing out, 'It otter be a good day!'

"I wonder how long it'll be before the otter puns get old," Kira chuckled, then pushed from the bed to use the little bathroom tucked in the corner of the studio apartment above the gallery. Though, Aislinn had tried to insist that Kira move into the house next door and live in her childhood bedroom, Kira had wanted her space. She'd always loved the studio space above the gallery, and even though half of it was used as a makeshift studio for Aislinn – it wasn't uncommon for her to run upstairs in the middle of the day and start painting – there was also a bed tucked under the eaves in the corner. Kira was used to packing light and didn't need much, so it had been an ideal solution for her. Plus, half of her clothes still resided in her old bedroom next door, so she could always run over and restock as necessary.

Ducking her head under the warm water, Kira thought about the otter Instagram page and how quickly it had taken off. It was unusual for something like that to grow that fast, and now she wondered if it was the universe giving her a little nudge to see this through. Perhaps she needed the affirmation – or even, frankly, the permission – that it was okay to stay in one spot for a change and settle into a project.

Granted, she certainly hoped it wouldn't be a long-term thing, this helping of the otters – she wanted to find a solution for Fergal quickly. But until she got a better idea of the lay of the land and specifically what developers were in the area, there wasn't much she could do but drum up virtual support for the battle she'd potentially have on her hands down the road.

For now, though, she needed a strong cup of coffee and a bite to eat before work. Towel-drying her curls, she piled them on top of her head under a loose-knit cap. In a mood today, she lined her eyes with a deep green liner, smudging them until they looked just edgy enough, and then hooked some large silver lightning-bolt-shaped earrings into her ears. Buttoning up a tartan shirt, she knotted it at the waist, then pulled on thick black leggings before slipping on thigh-high patent leather boots. Grabbing her slouchy leather bag, she threw it over her shoulder and clambered down the steps behind the shop, her mind on a proper fry-up and what to do about the otters. It wasn't until after she'd placed her to-go order at Ann's Café – and had a chat with Ann herself about everything from when she was getting married to who'd just had a baby – that Kira found herself glancing around the little diner.

Startled blue eyes met hers, and Kira felt a flash of heat move through her at the sight of the man sitting in an armchair by the little fireplace in the corner. Well, well, well, she thought. Things were looking up.

"That's grand, Ann," Kira responded, taking the bag the woman handed her and not even listening to what she was saying. "I'll be back in soon enough."

Kira crossed the room, nodding her hellos at a few people, and came to stand by the handsome man she'd met the other day.

"You've decided to stay on then," Kira said, shifting so her hip leaned against a table near his chair.

"Ah, yes, that was the plan all along." The man cleared his throat and offered her a smile.

"And how are you finding things?"

"Um, well, nice, that is. Everyone's very nice." His cheeks flushed a bit, and Kira was surprised to see a hint of distress cross his face.

"I'm Kira, by the way. I didn't catch your name the other day."

"My name's Brogan. A pleasure to meet you."

"And it's a pleasure to be meeting you as well, Brogan." Kira gave him one of her slow sexy grins and crossed her legs. When his eyes darted down to her legs and then back to her face, Kira let her smile widen.

"Your food," Brogan said.

"My food?"

"Um, your food. It's getting cold. I'm keeping you," Brogan said. He shifted awkwardly in his chair and the sheaf of papers on his lap tumbled to the floor.

"Oh, let me," Kira said, dropping her bag of food on the table and crouching to help. When her forehead hit Brogan's with a resounding thump, she sat back on her bum for a moment.

"Oh my god. I'm so sorry. Are you all right then?" Brogan's hands came to her face and he held her there, studying her forehead. His touch instantly electrified her, and despite her forehead smarting with pain, Kira licked her lips. When Brogan's gaze dropped to her mouth, the moment drew out.

"Is everyone all right? Are you needing some ice there, Kira?" Ann hurried over, worrying a dishtowel with her hands.

"No, I'll be fine. I've taken worse bumps on the head scrambling around these hills." Kira smiled and eased shakily back from a shocked-looking Brogan.

"Sir, are you well?" Ann asked, as Brogan had yet to move or speak.

"Oh, right. I'm just fine." Brogan shook his head, as if coming out of a fog, and hurriedly picked up his papers.

"It wasn't too hard of a hit. Just clumsy of me, is all." Kira stood and brushed off her leggings. "But I'm glad I put my coffee down first."

"Oh, that would've stung, wouldn't it?" Ann nodded.

"I'll be on my way then." Kira didn't think it was best to linger with a clearly embarrassed Brogan. If she knew anything about the male ego, it was that they didn't like looking foolish. "It was nice to run into you, Brogan."

"Literally," he murmured.

Kira threw her head back and laughed.

"Yes, quite literally. Hopefully, next time will be equally as impactful." Leaving that to sit with him as it would, Kira picked up her food and strolled out of the café humming to herself. If she wasn't wrong, Brogan was not unaffected by her presence. Which meant her stay here might just get a little more interesting.

Humming the whole way back to the shop, Kira smiled at everyone she passed, and was grateful that there was no rain to be had on this cool morning. She pushed the back door to the gallery open and looked to where Morgan was wrapping a painting.

Beautiful in a way that made people stop in their tracks, Morgan was one of the rare people who was unaffected by her looks. It was almost as if she didn't have a mirror, Kira thought, but loved her the more for being such an open-hearted soul. Morgan often kept people at arm's length, but those she let in she loved with a fierceness that would have made her warrior ancestors proud.

"You look cheerful this morning."

"I am. And I brought you a muffin." Kira put the bag down and pulled out two lemon poppyseed muffins. Though she'd wanted a proper fry-up for breakfast, she'd changed her mind when the delicious scent of Ann's baking had tantalized her.

"Have I mentioned how much I love having you here?" Morgan finished wrapping the painting and crossed the room to plop down on a chair.

"You have, but I'm always open to flattery."

"I'll keep it up if you promise to stay longer," Morgan

said, flashing her a grin before taking a bite of her muffin. She gave a little hum of pleasure at the taste.

"Seems to be the theme lately. I didn't realize how short of help you were here," Kira said, leaning against the counter. She took a sip of coffee and studied the gallery. It had a nice flow, she thought, the racks of smaller prints funneled people through to a bigger space where larger works of art were displayed on textured wood walls. Kira particularly enjoyed the local artists' corner, where they carried an ever-changing display of different mediums of art. The space was homey, yet chic, and it was rare for someone to visit without buying something. With a wide range of price points, the gallery had something for everyone.

"We aren't short of help. We just miss you," Morgan said.

"Well, that's very sweet. But I'm sure there are other people who can do this job just fine."

"There are, but you're an artist as well. And you bring a fresh eye to things. Look what you did with that display yesterday." Morgan gestured to where Kira had rearranged several paintings and a display of earrings to meld together. "You've brought sort of a funky edge to it. I like it."

"I'm glad. I was just fussing about."

"You're welcome to keep fussing. It's good to change things up. But for now, let's get through these online orders."

The day passed quickly. Kira had always known her mother's galleries were successful, but she hadn't realized just how busy they actually were, particularly with their online orders. Kira estimated that a good seventy percent of the sales they'd made that day were from the online shop alone.

"You can head off now, if you'd like. I'll close up," Morgan said mid-afternoon. She paused and stretched her arms over her head, then shook out the long hair that tumbled over her shoulders.

"You're sure? I can stay."

"No, it's fine. I'm going to meet Niamh for dinner."

"Is she home then? Tell her hi for me and to call me."

"I will, at that. She's home from college for a bit." Niamh, Morgan's daughter, was finishing out her last year at university. Kira could only imagine what she would do in the world, for Morgan's daughter was brilliant, boisterous, and full of magick. It would be fun to watch her make her mark.

"Great. I'll catch up with her soon enough then." Kira waved goodbye and pounded up the stairs to her studio. There was just enough daylight left that she could hike out to visit Fergal and see if she could get any more photos for Instagram, and maybe drive the area a bit and see if she could locate this construction.

Switching out her patent leather boots for her hiking boots, Kira grabbed her coat and her camera, and shoved a few cereal bars and a water bottle into her pack. She picked up her keys, and in moments she was navigating the twisty road that hugged the cliffs along the water. She loved this drive, even if it was slower and more inconvenient than the straight road that shot over the hills.

Sometimes the slower path offered opportunities for moments of inspiration or beauty.

$\mathcal{K}$ira bypassed Gracie's cottage, following a dirt road that wound further into the hills, so as to get closer to the starting point for her hike. Yesterday, she'd taken the time to wander about, but with the waning light it was important that she get to Fergal's little pond quickly to see if she could get any good images for her new Instagram account. Plus, she just wanted to check on him. A cussing otter was something she had not expected to come across, and his cheekiness pleased her mightily.

Getting out of the car, Kira wound a scarf around her neck and zipped her jacket against the sharp needles of cold hammered against her by the wind. Up in the hills it was much colder than in the village, but Kira, having walked these hills her whole life, was prepared for the change in temperature. It wasn't uncommon for the weather to switch from sunshine to rain and back again in minutes, and today was just such a day. Grateful that the clouds had yet to open up and it was just cold she was dealing with, Kira trudged up the dirt path, skirting the boulders easily.

Kira reached the pond quickly, and let out a little sigh of contentment. The cliff walls that rose behind the pond blocked a large portion of the wind, creating a zen-like oasis of mossy green ground and still mountain waters. Pleased to see a ripple move across the pond, Kira immediately crouched and brought the camera at her neck to her eye, firing off a round of shots as the otter floated across the water like he didn't have a care in the world. When he reached the edge of the pond, he paused and tilted his head at her.

Friend.

"Hi, Fergal. I came back to see you."

Friend.

"Yes, I'm your friend. I brought you something." Kira opened a little baggie of fresh fish she'd snagged from Morgan's lunch.

Food.

"Yes, food."

The otter scampered over to her and grabbed the fish from her hands before moving a careful distance away. Kira relaxed into position, comfortable in her crouch; she was used to angling her body in weird ways to get the shot she wanted. She took round after round of photos, knowing she'd have plenty to choose from for her account later.

Shite! Man!

Kira jumped up and whirled around as Fergal dropped his food and dived into the pond.

"I'm sorry. I didn't mean to scare him. He seemed quite friendly."

Kira paused as she recognized Brogan. He must have already been out on the land, as Kira hadn't passed any other cars on her way here. Brogan smiled as he made his way around the pond. He looked confident here, she realized, in a way that he hadn't in the store. He wore a red coat and a faded grey knit cap, the ends of his hair curling out from beneath. He looked rugged and handsome, and like someone Kira definitely wanted to get to know better.

Without thinking, she held her camera up and took a few photos of him before he realized what she was doing and stopped walking to smile foolishly at her.

"Sorry, it's habit," Kira said.

"Would you like me to pose?" Brogan cocked an arm at his waist and lifted a hand in the air like a model.

"That works." Kira laughed and took a few shots, and Brogan immediately dropped his arm, an embarrassed look on his handsome face.

"I didn't think you'd actually take the photos."

"Well, I'm a photographer. It's second nature." Kira shrugged and stood, stretching her legs, then hopped up on a boulder. As Brogan approached her, she kept an eye on Fergal, who was watching them from the pond.

"Is that your art form then? You did mention you were an artist the other day," Brogan said as he stopped in front of her.

So he remembered their conversation. Kira smiled to herself.

"Yes, I'm a photographer."

"Nature then? I saw you taking photos of the otter. He's quite cute. I haven't seen any others, though."

"Nature, among other things. I'm a bit scattered in my work. I've never liked being boxed into one genre. I've taken photos of dignitaries, musicians, and animals in the African wilds. It really just depends what opportunity I'm presented with, and what strikes my fancy."

"And today, it's otters."

"Today, it's otters." Kira grinned at Brogan and patted the boulder next to her. "Come sit with me. We can have a chat with the otter and learn more about him. I've called him Fergal."

"That's a strong name." Brogan hoisted himself onto the boulder. They were close enough that she could feel his heat, but not quite touching.

"I thought so. He seems to like it."

"How do you know that?"

"He told me," Kira said, knowing immediately that Brogan would dismiss her. Most people did when she told them she could commune with animals.

"Is that right? What else did he have to say?" Brogan's eyes crinkled at the corners when he smiled at her, and Kira couldn't help but smile back.

"He's worried for his home. There's developers nearby that are hurting the stream of water that comes through."

"I... um." Brogan took a moment to look around and then back to her. Kira just gave him a pleasant smile and looked away, letting him come to his own conclusions. She didn't mind if people thought she was weird – though she suspected she might have just killed her chance for a quick shag with Brogan while he was in town.

The silence between them drew out. Kira kept taking photos of Fergal, who had grown more comfortable with Brogan's presence and returned to the side of the pond to eat the rest of his snack.

"What brings you up here, Brogan?" Kira shifted the conversation to a safe topic. "It's a long ways out for someone just passing through the town."

"Oh, well, I like being in nature. I'm probably more comfortable here than anywhere else."

"Not a big city guy?"

"I mean, they certainly have their uses. But I like the quiet. Though nature is hardly quiet, is it? Just listen – the bird calls on the wind, the waves hitting the cliffs down below, the splash of the water as Fergal dives under. It has its own song, nature does." Brogan snapped his mouth shut and a faint flush crossed his cheeks.

"You're a romantic, are you then?" Kira smiled as the flush deepened on his cheeks. "Well, I happen to agree with you there. I do love exploring – big cities or rambling fields – but I tend to gravitate toward nature as well."

"That surprises me, I'll admit. I wouldn't have... I mean... I certainly wasn't expecting... well..." Brogan ran a hand over his face.

"You didn't think a woman who wears patent leather thigh-high boots would also don a pair of hiking boots and tromp through the mud?"

"Precisely," Brogan sighed. "And I do realize that sounds rude."

"It's okay. I like when people underestimate me."

"That I certainly haven't done, I can promise you that," Brogan said.

"Well, I like when people don't know what to expect from me, how about that? It's good to keep people on their toes." Kira turned and took a few more photos. "I like fashion, but I'm also practical. And if I'm going to get muddy and wet in nature, it's not going to be in my expensive boots."

"Smart."

"Precisely." Kira smiled as Fergal approached them, his nose lifted to the wind to scent them. "I think he's starting to trust you."

"Is he? I would hope so. I mean him no harm."

Friend?

"Yes, he's a friend." Kira kept her eyes on Fergal, though she knew Brogan had turned to watch her.

Shite.

"He's not shite. He's a friend."

"Did he just swear at me?"

Kira shrugged. "Apparently, he learned it from a builder on the construction site."

"You're having me on, aren't you?" Brogan cracked a smile at her.

Kira turned and tilted her head to meet his eyes. Thick lashes rimmed intense blue eyes, and she didn't read ridicule there. Brogan was genuinely curious.

"No, I'm not. I can communicate with animals."

"Like... how, exactly? You get images in your mind? Or you can speak with them? Because he didn't make any sound at you or anything. So I can't quite fathom how you're translating otter-language."

Kira threw back her head and laughed, delighted with Brogan and his observations. At least he hadn't run screaming, she thought, or talked down to her. Patting his arm, she met his eyes again.

"I like you, Brogan."

"Well, um, thank you. I like you, too," Brogan said quickly.

"I'm not sure that you do. Yet. But you will." Kira smiled and turned back to look at Fergal. "To answer your question, no, I don't translate their language. Their words just kind of show up in my brain. Like I can read them on a chalkboard in my mind. I suppose it would be like being able to read someone's mind, except for me, it's animals."

"Have you always been able to do this?"

"Pretty much. My Mam took it more seriously when I was about four and having full-on conversations with the cat."

"I'm sure the cat loved that."

"You know what? He really did. I loved that cat." Kira sighed and put her hand to her heart. "Broke my heart when he passed on."

"It's the hardest thing about having animals," Brogan agreed.

"You don't seem put off by this. Most people make fun of me." Kira leaned in a bit and pressed her shoulder against his, testing him. When he didn't move back, she took that as a win.

"I try not to make fun of things I don't understand. I suppose that's the scientist in me. I like to ask questions. Figure things out. But just because I don't understand something doesn't mean it's wrong or bad. I hope you don't mind if I ask more questions, though."

"So long as I get to ask a few questions of my own."

"Go ahead."

"What kind of scientist are you?"

"I'm an environmental scientist. Land use and the like. Looking for ways we can co-exist with nature instead of hurting it."

"That's nice. Perhaps you can be of some help with the construction guys who are bothering Fergal."

"I can help look into it. How... can you show me how you talk to him?"

Kira slanted a glance at Brogan and then made chattering noises at the otter. When Fergal bounced closer and glared at her, it took everything in her power to not laugh.

That's shite.

"What's happening? What did you say?" Brogan breathed.

Kira let out a loud whoop and slapped her palm on her knee. "I'm just teasing with you. I told you, I don't have to speak their language. I can just talk normally. I don't know how it gets translated or transmitted to them. It just does."

"Oh." Brogan shook his head and laughed. "You had me."

"Fergal, this is my friend, Brogan."

Friend.

"Yes, friend. Can you show him that you understand me? Maybe... let's see." Kira looked down at Brogan's shoes. "Can you run up and grab one of his shoelaces? Maybe he'll believe me then."

Do you have more food?

"Yes, I have more food."

Fine.

Kira watched Brogan's eyes widen as the otter scam-

pered over and tugged on one of Brogan's shoelaces. He
pulled the knot completely apart before sitting back to look
up at Kira.

"Great job. I think he believes me. Here's some more
food." Kira took more out of her pouch and handed it to
the little otter. He took it from her hands and scampered
back to the water.

"He just untied my shoelaces. Because you told
him to."

Kira wondered if this was the part where he would go
running. It wouldn't be the first time.

"Aye, that's correct."

"You're amazing." Brogan beamed at her.

Kira felt warmth rush through her. Acting on impulse,
as she had done for much of her life, Kira leaned forward
and pressed her lips to his.

A zip of energy hummed between them for a moment,
shocking Kira's eyes open. Then, with a crack of thunder,
the skies opened up and pounded them with rain.

CHAPTER 8

*S*he'd kissed him.

It was hours later, and Brogan shook his head as he toweled off from his desperately needed hot shower. They'd run their separate ways when the storm hit, since their cars were parked far away from each other. At the time, it had been instinctual, but now Brogan wondered what she'd thought of him taking off like that. Granted, it had been a nasty storm that had whipped up out of nowhere – still, Brogan berated himself for not running with Kira to her car to make sure she got there safely.

He hadn't been thinking clearly. Her kiss… well, it had shocked him. Brogan brought a hand to his lips where he could've sworn he still felt the heat from her lips. Had she felt the same thing he had?

Or maybe she'd put a spell on him.

Brogan muttered an expletive as he ran the towel over his hair. He wouldn't be Irish if he hadn't heard his fair share of stories about the fae and magickal realms. In fact, his own gran had insisted that the very land she'd bequeathed him was magickal. He'd always entertained her stories, never once letting her believe that he questioned her thoughts. He'd thought it charming that she believed in magick. He didn't, of course – it warred with his scientific outlook. But his gran had done no harm with her beliefs and they had brought her joy – so Brogan had seen no need to try and change her mind.

You've a kind heart, Brogan.

He could still hear the words his gran had spoken as she lay on her deathbed. He'd sat with her during her final days and listened as she'd rambled on, telling him of enchanted waters and blood magick passed down through generations. But in the end, she'd held his hand and thanked him for always listening to her, even though she knew he didn't believe in the same things she did. It had meant a lot to him, knowing that he could bring her some comfort in her last days.

His own mother surely hadn't.

Brogan's mother, Dorothea, was a vapid, sullen woman who had wanted the world to be handed to her on a silken cushion. Furious that she'd had to work for a living, Dorothea had allowed her bitterness to poison both herself and all of her relationships. It was a miracle that Brogan hadn't inherited the toxic traits from her – likely due to the fact that he always wanted to be out of the house. He had spent hours roaming the hills as a young lad, forever searching for reasons to stay away from home.

He had created many a magickal story in those days. He'd built forts with imaginary friends, and won fierce battles in the woods with others. With a vivid imagination and inquisitive mind, he'd grown to love the natural world;

from that, his quest to know more, more, *more* had blossomed. Grateful for his gran, who had been the one to encourage him in science, Brogan had found his own tentative path.

Away from his mother.

She'd become enraged when his gran's will was read. Dorothea had been convinced for years that she would inherit Gran's land and money. But when she saw that the will had listed only Brogan's name, Dorothea had spit on his shoes. Six months later, she'd died from late-stage liver cancer, having refused Brogan's calls to the last day of her life.

And that just about summed up everything there was to know about his upbringing. Now, he sought the solace of the outdoors and a desire to learn more about this land that his gran had loved so much. Maybe, just maybe, he could feel closer to her by spending time here.

It also helped that Gran had been loaded, which meant Brogan could afford to take time off work.

To look at her, one would never have guessed she was rich as could be. She wore her clothes until they were threadbare, insisting on patching every hole, and the only jewelry she'd worn was the gold band her husband had given her on their wedding day. His gran had lived a simple life, rich in nature and friendships, and he'd been astonished at the sum she'd left to him along with the land.

It had given Brogan some freedom to decide what his next steps in life were. His last project for a coastal waterways project had ended recently. He had a pile of inquiries for other environmental assessment projects, but had decided to put himself on a self-imposed sabbatical instead of automatically taking the next job that came his way. Now, he'd finally decided to visit the land his gran had left to him.

Thus far, he'd learned two things from his self-imposed break from work.

One was that he wanted to do better in the world.

And the second, and more surprising one, was that he wanted to have a family. It had hit him like a lightning bolt one day. The thought still shocked him, because he couldn't remember ever seriously wanting a family before.

It had been a sunny day in Kinsale, and Brogan was lingering over a pint at a picnic table tucked outside a local pub. A young couple, surely a few years younger than him, had sat at another table with their rosy-cheeked child, who was still finding his feet. Brogan had been amused at the way the child had toddled to his parents and fallen on his bum before he reached them. The mother had picked the baby up and cuddled him close, while the man had wrapped an arm around her shoulders.

I want that.

The thought had stopped him in his tracks. Perhaps it was because, growing up, he'd never had that easy affection in his own family. His mother had been more likely to swat his bum than to cuddle him if he'd had a bad dream. Brogan's childhood home had always been filled with tension, and his days had felt like he was constantly navigating a field chock full of landmines. From an early age, he'd convinced himself he'd never wanted a family, and instead, had thrown himself into his studies.

Why was he thinking about this now? Brogan dressed and crossed to the little kitchenette in his gran's cottage.

Initially, he had thought to stay in the village of Grace's Cove, but there was something about being out in the middle of nowhere, where the only other lights he could see were the stars, that deeply appealed to the hermit in him right now. Opening the little cool box, he studied its contents before deciding that tonight he would take Liam up on the offer of a beer. Not that he was going to call him and ask him – oh no, that sounded too much like a date. Instead, he'd just pop down to the pub and see if Liam was around. If not, he'd get a bite to eat and wander on home.

With that decided, Brogan shoved thoughts of wanting a family – and of his kiss with Kira – out of his head. It wouldn't do to mull over things that weren't likely to happen. He needed to spend more time figuring out what he wanted to do with his life and less time thinking about a witchy-eyed woman with a riot of curls he wanted to dive his hands into.

Gallagher's Pub was lit up cheerfully with two lanterns beside the entrance and light glowing through the windows. Brogan had passed it several times, but this would be his first time stepping through the doors. Taking a deep breath and pushing his shoulders back, as he always did before entering a crowded space, Brogan pushed the door open and automatically scanned the room.

To his left, a long wooden bar, polished to a gleaming shine in the overhead lights, stretched the length of one wall. Glass shelves lined a mirrored wall above the bar, and a pint-sized woman bustled about behind the bar hollering orders. To his right, booths ran along both walls, and tables had been pushed aside for an impromptu dance session. Two young girls bounced to a jaunty Irish tune, played by a handful of musicians who had shoehorned themselves into a corner booth.

Brogan could see why this space was the heart of the town, for young and old alike to share. With a smile, he turned to make his way to the bar.

"Brogan! There's a lad. Come join us."

Brogan turned to see Liam at a table with another man. He crossed to them and took the seat that Liam had pulled out.

"Brogan, this is my best mate and worst boss, Dylan."

"He's lying." Dylan flashed a smile at Brogan.

"About the best mate part?" Brogan asked.

Liam slapped his hand on the table and laughed.

"Oh, he's a comedian then? Just what we need," Dylan grumbled, but Brogan could tell he wasn't angry.

"Nice to meet you both."

"I'm glad you came out. How have you been?" Liam asked.

Brogan paused as the tiny, and slightly terrifying, woman from behind the bar zipped to their table with two pints of Guinness in her hands.

"And who's this, then?"

"Cait, this is Brogan. He's new to town," Liam said.

Cait paused and studied Brogan, and his shoulders tensed. It was almost as if there was an unnatural probing into his head. Was his mind playing tricks on him?

Cait narrowed her eyes. "You've the look of someone I know. You from around here?"

"My gran was."

"Her name?"

"Catherine Brogan O'Hallahan." Brogan had inherited his gran's maiden name as his first.

"Get out! She was good friends with Fiona, though Fiona was much older. They didn't live all that far from each other. Are you here to clear out her cottage then?"

"Um, not sure. I'm staying there, yes. But I don't believe I'll do much clearing. She led a pretty simple life and the stuff she had is still quite nice and in good repair."

"That's a good lad. I'm sick of people always tossing out useful things."

"Aye, I understand. Some of the things built generations ago last longer than stuff made today."

"That's the truth of it." Cait pointed a finger at him. "What can I get you? First pint's on me."

"I'm driving."

"Tea?"

"Sure, that's grand. And do you have a menu?"

"Special tonight is Irish stew with homemade bread. I've got a bread pudding for dessert as well."

"Sounds perfect for a cold night."

Cait was gone before he finished speaking and Brogan shook his head slightly. Though she was little, her presence was large, and it seemed to take him a moment to recalibrate himself once she'd left their table.

"You'll get used to it. Cait runs a tight ship, but she's got a huge heart," Liam said.

"We're all a little scared of Cait."

"I heard that," Cait called, and Dylan hunched his shoulders.

"See?" Liam whispered from the side of his mouth.

"I like her," Brogan laughed.

"Good. Best to stay on her good side. So, you've roots here then? Where's the cottage exactly?" Dylan asked, taking a long sip of his pint.

"Up the cliffs. Past the cottage right by the cove."

"That's our cottage. Well, it's Gracie's, but she's kindly allowed me to share it with her."

"Gracie is Dylan's wife. They met when he threatened to bulldoze her cottage down." Liam smiled and elbowed Dylan in the ribs.

"You did not." Brogan's mouth hung open.

"Oh, he did. And we about strung him up for it." Cait materialized at their table again and put a pot of tea in front of Brogan.

"But you've since forgiven me," Dylan reminded her.

"I've still got eyes on you." Cait sniffed and disappeared again.

"That woman can hold a grudge."

"Show me one that can't," Liam said.

"He's not wrong," Dylan agreed.

"I'm assuming you were persuaded to change your mind, since the cottage is still standing?" Brogan asked.

"Aye. I was shown the error of my ways. And was gifted the love of my life along the way. So, win-win."

"That's grand it all worked out. The cottage looks to be in great shape. It would have been a shame to lose it," Brogan said.

"How's your gran's cottage?" Liam asked.

"It's nice. She truly took good care of it, so there's little in the way of maintenance for me to do."

"What's your plan? Will you sell it? That's a lot of land with the cottage if I recall correctly." Dylan leaned back and studied Brogan. "In fact, if I think back, I believe she was the majority landholder in that area. Which means…"

"Which means what?" Liam looked from Dylan to Brogan.

"What are your plans for the land again?" Dylan asked, casting a quick look at Liam, who promptly shut his mouth.

"No plans at the moment. I just came over to actually see it. I don't think I was truly aware of just how much land she owned either. When I visited, I mainly stayed in the hills surrounding her cottage. It wasn't until her will was read that I had any notion of the expanse of her property."

"It's a fair parcel, I'll give you that." Dylan took another sip of his pint and studied Brogan.

"Yes. Though, I have to ask how you're knowing that."

"It's what I do. Development. Land, businesses, shipping companies…" Dylan shrugged. "I'm in the way of being aware of what's about the area, is all."

"Ah, I understand. Particularly as it borders your land now."

"Wait a minute. This makes more sense now." Liam nodded at Brogan. "I know what you're here for."

"You do?" Brogan looked at Liam in surprise, wondering what he was thinking.

"Aye, you're the one ripping up the land for a fancy new housing development. Which isn't really needed at all."

CHAPTER 9

"*H*elp me come up with an otter joke."

"You otter be kidding me."

"I'm not. I need a caption," Kira grumbled, glaring at her phone.

"No. That was the pun. 'You otter be'... like 'gotta be' but 'otter'?" Gracie sighed and shook her head sadly at Kira.

"Oh. Duh." Kira shook her own head and laughed at Gracie. "I guess my mind is elsewhere. I should've gotten that."

"You have been a little spacey this morning. And... yet." Gracie settled back in an old wooden rocking chair that was tucked into an alcove of her living room. Rosie snored on her soft mat in front of the fire while Kira had curled herself into a padded armchair next to Gracie. Kira had the day off from the gallery and had come out to spend a relaxed morning with Grace. It wasn't often she was home with no agenda, so it was nice to just sit with a cup of tea and chat with a friend.

"And yet?" Kira looked up from her phone.

"You've been distracted. But also humming to yourself. If I didn't know better, I'd say you had yourself a shag."

"Not quite a shag, but –"

"What!" Gracie screeched, making Rosie hop up from her pillow. "You shagged someone and didn't tell me?"

"I just said it wasn't a shag."

"Who is this man? I must know. I haven't even gotten through my list. Is this the mysterious stranger from the store?"

"It is. And I kissed him. No shagging. Just a kiss."

"Oh la la," Gracie trilled. "And why no shagging?"

"Because I'm not that kind of girl?" Kira raised an eyebrow at Grace. The moment stretched out in silence until they both collapsed in laughter.

"Fine. *Sometimes* I'm that kind of girl. But I kissed him on impulse because he was being incredibly sweet and not running screaming for the hills when I told him I could talk to animals. Then a storm exploded over our heads, we both ran for our cars, and I haven't seen him since."

"And this was how long ago?"

"Two days ago."

"Hmm. And he didn't stop by the gallery to try and find you?"

"Nope." Kira sniffed. If the man was interested, surely, he would have come by to see about a date.

"Maybe he's been busy."

"Maybe. Or perhaps he's just not interested," Kira said.

"Impossible. You're fantastic."

"Well, *you* know that. But he doesn't know that yet." Kira fluttered her eyelashes at Gracie.

"Fine, take me out of it. Anyone can see – from an objective standpoint, that is – that you're an interesting person. You dress like you actually like your body. You wear unique pieces, you have a camera hanging around your neck more often than not, you smile easily, and you're genuinely a flexible and easygoing person. That shines through whether I know you or not. And I think those are traits that most men would be interested in – or at the very least, come back for a second taste of."

"Well then." A warm flush of love filled Kira. "I love you. You're so good for my soul."

"I'm not saying you can't be a bitch, mind," Gracie said, and laughed when Kira reached over and swatted her. "See? That's not nice."

"Coming from Queen Bitch herself," Kira muttered into her teacup.

"And don't you be forgetting it, now."

"How could I? You remind me constantly."

Gracie narrowed her eyes at Kira, who blew a kiss in her direction.

"What's this lad's name again?" Gracie asked, changing the subject neatly.

"Brogan."

"Oh!" Gracie sat up and looked at Kira, alarm written across her pretty features. "That's right! The lad Dylan met in the pub the other night! Sorry, I've been right scatter-brained lately – I forgot all about it."

"Did he now? Do tell," Kira said.

"Kira, I don't think it's good. Dylan seems to think he's developing the land."

"Wait, what?" A slice of apprehension laced through Kira. "What do you mean?"

"His gran used to be friends with Fiona. The cottage along the way over the hills? To the back of us?" Gracie waved her hand vaguely toward the back of her cottage. "You know the one?"

"Aye, I do."

"That's his gran's cottage. She passed last year and I guess he's come to see to the land. She owned clear to the other side of the peninsula. And there's builders on the land now to make that fancy new housing development. For what? I don't know. Nobody living out here is that fancy. I think they're trying to attract the super-rich as like a vacation hotspot, but don't you think they'd miss out on the charm of Ireland if they're tucked away in some fancy new-build construction? What about the history? And the nature? No, it can't be good."

"Wait, back up." Kira waved away Grace's questions about what the super-rich wanted on their holidays. "You're saying that Brogan is behind the new development that's going on in the area?"

"I think so. It's on his land, from my understanding. Dylan said he protested that it wasn't his. But Liam said he saw Brogan looking at land use management studies when he was working at Ann's Café. So it has to be him."

"Land use... I saw the same. When we collided at the café."

"You collided?"

"Bumped heads. He dropped his papers and we

reached down at the same time. Those *were* land studies."
Fury ripped through Kira. How dare this man come to their
land and try to turn it into a development? And here he'd
been playing all cute with the otters too. She curled her
fists together, forcing herself to breathe before she did
something drastic.

"I can't believe I was so wrong about him. He seemed
to genuinely care about nature. And his aura was good. Is
that possible? Can my magick misfire like that?"

"Tell me everything and we'll go from there," Gracie
said, slanting a look at a bottle of whiskey on the shelf. "Is
it too early for whiskey?"

"Not if it's in coffee," Kira said.

"I've got heavy cream for it too. Let's go to the kitchen
and break this down. Because I do trust your instincts and
your magick. I feel like you'd know if he was a bad
person."

"For sure, I would be knowing that," Kira huffed. She
took the metal bowl of cream from Gracie and sat down at
the long bench that lined the massive wooden kitchen table
where Gracie mixed her potions and tinctures. Needing
something to do with her energy, Kira began to ferociously
whisk the cream.

"What was his aura energy?" Gracie asked as she
measured the coffee.

"Blue and green. It was really a lovely aura, which is
what actually interested me at first. I thought, for once, I
could enjoy a fling with a nice guy."

"Hmm, what was Dax's?"

"Jax. It was brown and red." Kira hung her head.

"Shame on you." Gracie tsked. "You know better."

A brown aura typically suggested someone who was selfish and a red aura would indicate someone driven by passion. Mixing them together would make someone who was incredibly focused on one particular thing. In Jax's case, it was himself and his music. Not exactly a winning combination for someone as a partner, but it was what had made him successful as a rock star.

"I know, I know, I know." Kira handed Gracie back the bowl of cream. "But it was what made him incredibly good at what he does. And it was also what made me take notice when I found an attractive man with a decidedly different aura."

"That's fine then. So say your aura reading is right – what's going on, then?" Gracie poured a generous splash of whiskey in each coffee and added a dollop of cream on top. Turning, she came to sit next to Kira and handed her a steaming glass. "Sláinte."

"Maybe... maybe he thinks he *is* doing a good thing? That he's bringing tourists to the area and infusing the economy with money? I mean, I guess he's giving locals jobs, too."

"He's not, though. The locals are working for Dylan on the community center. Remember how people were grumbling over the fact that a new company had brought people in?"

"Oh right, I did hear something about that." Kira licked the cream from around the rim of the cup and took her first sip of the coffee. It was a perfect mix, and just what a blustery day on the cliffs called for.

"Tell me about your kiss."

"Well, it was an impulse on my part. I've been going up to visit the otters like I told you about."

Gracie nodded and motioned for Kira to continue.

"Which is why I've started this otter Instagram. I wanted to raise support and awareness that their habitats are being threatened. Plus, they're so damn cute."

"They really are."

"And I was up at the pond in the hills and…" Kira stopped and smacked her palm to her forehead. "Of course, now it makes sense why Brogan was up there. I thought it was an odd spot to find him wandering about."

"It's his land. The otters are on *his* land."

"It is. Wow, okay, he never said a thing. He didn't tell me I was on his land."

"What did you talk about?"

"Mmm, otters. Photography. That kind of thing. He's an environmental scientist."

"Is he? Is that a fancy way of saying he studies how to build on the land?"

"I feel like the two would be different, but now I have no idea what to think." Kira sighed and rolled her shoulders back to ease some of the tension that was gathering there.

"Okay, so you talked about work and otters. I'm still failing to understand how such a riveting discussion led to a kiss."

Kira glared at Gracie, who just raised an eyebrow at her.

"Now who's the bitchy one?"

"I've always been the bitchy one. Have you met me?" Gracie laughed and tossed her head, much like a thoroughbred tossing its mane. "Now, in all seriousness. How did talking about otters lead to a kiss?"

"Well, you know I'm open with my gifts. So I just told him that I was talking to the otter. And he didn't run screaming. Fergal was kind enough to demonstrate that I'm not mental and actually *can* speak to animals, and Brogan took it in his stride."

"Fergal?"

"Oh, my otter friend. I named him. Did you know otters can cuss? He learned it from the construction guys."

"I… I did not. Oh no – that means Rosie probably can too!"

At her name, the dog walked over to the bench and swung her head between the two of them.

Food?

"No food just now. Gracie wants to know if you can cuss."

Bloody hell. F–

"That's enough," Kira laughed, cutting Rosie off. "Yes, she can curse."

"I can't imagine where she learned that from." Gracie pointed her nose in the air. "I'll have to speak to Dylan about his language."

"Dylan. *Right*," Kira muttered to Rosie and reached down to pet the dog's silken ears.

"I think what we need to focus on here is that you kissed Brogan because of… an otter?"

"I kissed him because we were having a companionable moment sitting on a boulder together. I kissed him because I told him I could talk to animals and he wasn't mean to me. I kissed him because I wanted to see his reaction. And, I guess… mine too."

"And what was yours?"

"Agh, Gracie, that's the thing. It felt good. Like really good. Like… my whole body lit up from within. I swear I felt a zap or a zing or something just shoot straight through me. It shocked me so much that I'm not sure what I would've done if the storm hadn't broke."

"Interesting timing, that."

"You think it was… what? The cove?"

"More likely Fiona." Grace shot a menacing look to the ceiling of the cottage in case Fiona was nearby.

"Why would she want to break the kiss up? If I felt so good about it?"

"That's the question that remains to be answered."

CHAPTER 10

*K*ira braced her shoulders against the wind. It buffeted down the hills as if trying to push her back from visiting what had quickly become her little oasis. She didn't care whose land it was. The pond and the otters now fell under her jurisdiction, as far as she was concerned, and she was going to make sure they were cared for. Trudging up the hill, her head bent, she tried to make sense of the thoughts that whirled through her mind.

It wasn't that she was *never* wrong about a person. It was just incredibly rare. Her instincts, combined with her magick, made it virtually impossible for anyone to trick her. Sure, there had been instances – like with Jax – when she hadn't made the best choices. But it wasn't because of lack of insight on her part; it was because she'd made a decision to ignore the red flags. That was an entirely different situation than being fooled by someone or misreading their aura.

Kira kept circling back to her conclusion that Brogan must think his development was doing something good for the area. That was the only thing that made sense to her. That, or her magick was blocked by lust. And, oh boy, did she have a healthy amount of lust roiling about for Brogan. She'd done nothing but think delightfully naughty thoughts about him since their kiss.

Or maybe she had just *really* wanted him to be a nice guy. Had her desire for a potential lover clouded her magick? Kira shook her head. Even though she'd been enthralled with Jax, she had still been well aware of her readings of him. And now she had an even bigger problem – not only did she have to save Fergal's habitat, she also had to confront Brogan.

Frustrated, Kira kicked at a stone in her path. "Nothing comes easily, does it," she muttered.

Friend.

"Hey there, Fergal," Kira crouched by the side of the pond and smiled at the otter, who paddled lazily about. She wondered where his friends and family were. Weren't otters supposed to be social animals? Kira put her camera to her eye and spent the next half hour wandering the edges of the pond, checking her light and adapting her angles to get the best possible shots of Fergal.

What are you doing?

"This is a camera. Um, it creates an image…a likeness of you. So that others can see it. Remember when I had this the other day? It's the same thing." Kira had never thought about having to explain what a camera or a photo-graph was; it was just accepted technology. Conversing with an otter, she thought, was kind of like conversing with an alien who had just landed on their planet and had no idea what anything was.

Food?

"I do have some for you today." Kira pulled out a foil-wrapped packet of fish and laid it gently on the side of the pond. Worry rushed through her for a moment. Should she even be feeding him? What if he expected her to bring food every day? "Fergal, you know I can't always bring you food, right? You still have to hunt on your own."

I know. But your food is easy.

"It is easy. But I can't promise to come here all the time. So please don't rely on me. Or other humans, for that matter. Not all of us can be trusted."

I know.

She supposed he probably had already learned that, depending on his experiences with the construction workers. The thought of Brogan's development made her grimace.

Man.

Fergal slid away from the fish and into the water, looking past Kira.

"I didn't expect to see you here again."

Her shoulders tensed as Brogan's voice cut across her calm oasis.

"And why's that?"

"I don't know. It's a long ways out, I guess," Brogan said, coming to stand next to her.

Feeling at a disadvantage in her crouched position, Kira stood and turned to Brogan. Surprise flitted through her as she noted the packet of fish in his hands.

"I like it here. It's calm. A serene oasis away from it all. Plus, Fergal tells great jokes."

"Does he now?" A smile bloomed on Brogan's face,

twisting a knot in Kira's stomach.

"No, I'm lying. And I told him not to rely on humans for food. Best not to be giving him any then." Kira sniffed and used her foot to try to cover the rest of the fish Fergal had left on the shoreline.

"Is that right? I could've sworn I saw you feeding the wee lad just moments ago."

"Be that as it may, best not to give him any more. He'll get fat."

I need fat for the winter.

"It's coming on spring, isn't it then, Fergal?" Kira glared at the otter, who had come back to the edge of the water, his head tilted up to eye the packet in Brogan's hands.

Still need food.

"Fine, go on then," Kira said with an annoyed wave. She moved away from where Brogan crouched to hand food to Fergal. The otter moved slowly with Brogan, taking his time, glancing over his shoulder every once in a while at Kira, whom he trusted. Kira bit her lip to keep from reassuring Fergal that Brogan wouldn't hurt him, because this development of his *was* hurting the otter's habitat and certainly Fergal would be able to tell she was lying. Animals were smart like that. They were more in tune to the frequencies of the universe, and could read tension in the air as easily as a seasoned sailor could predict a squall.

Kira walked around the edge of the pond and hunkered down with her back to a boulder to block the wind. Despite herself, Kira put the camera to her eye and fired off shot after shot of Brogan feeding Fergal. Her heart did a strange little shiver as she watched them both, the strong lines of the man bent over gently feeding the otter. He took his time with Fergal, allowing the otter to get used to him, and never once did he stir or startle the animal. It made Kira think that Brogan was comfortable in nature and respectful of animals. Which, again, was at odds with him bulldozing the land without a thought to the environment. Unsure of the mixed messages she was receiving, Kira worried her bottom lip as Brogan straightened and turned to her. Helpless not to, Kira raised the camera and took another photo of him. This shot, straight on, was one that Kira was certain she'd examine further later. Brogan's eyes creased at the corners as he smiled at her, and the wind whipped his hair around – he'd forgotten his cap. The urge to go to him, to wrap her arms around his waist and burrow into his warmth was almost too strong to ignore. Annoyed at her thoughts, Kira glared at Brogan.

"What's wrong?" Brogan stopped a few steps away and tilted his head at her in question.

"Why ever would you think something is wrong?" Kira asked.

"You just gave me a look like you wanted to strip me bare and run a dagger through my heart."

Kira shoved her thoughts away from stripping the man of his clothes, and pasted a smile on her face that she realized probably looked more like a snarl.

"That's not much better," Brogan said, confirming her thoughts. "I may not be an expert on women, but I can certainly tell when one is in a mood."

"I'm not too pleased with you," Kira said, standing up and leaning back against the boulder.

"With me?" A surprised look ran across Brogan's handsome face. "What have I done?"

"You're well aware of it," Kira said and then almost rolled her eyes at her words. She refused to be the kind of woman who danced around a subject and made a man jump through hoops to get an answer.

"I am?"

"The development," Kira clarified. She shifted, brushing a loose tendril of hair away from her face, and looked past Brogan to where Fergal happily pottered along the shoreline, picking up remnants of fish.

"I'm going to need you to be a bit clearer," Brogan said.

"The housing development."

"Ach, I told Dylan I've got nothing to do with that. Is he off spreading rumors about me then?" Brogan crossed his hands over his chest, his brow furrowed in frustration. "I was very clear that I had no idea what he was going on about."

"Yes, this is about the housing development. It's come to my attention that this is your land, is it not?" Kira lifted her chin at Brogan.

"Aye, this is now my land," Brogan agreed.

"Well, then it's also your development. I don't tolerate liars, Brogan."

For the first time, Kira saw a flash of anger race through Brogan, turning his aura a brilliant red before it returned back to its normal colors. Kira found herself pushing back against the boulder as Brogan strode forward, his face but inches from hers.

"Let me be very clear, Kira," Brogan said, anger lacing

his voice. "I am not a liar and I will not stand for people besmirching my honor."

Despite the anger in his words, Kira found her mouth quirking in a smile.

"That's very eighteen-hundreds of you, isn't it then? Besmirching his honor, himself says. Can you believe it?" Kira laughed.

"I'll not let you laugh this off." Brogan didn't move when Kira stepped forward.

Kira found herself dangerously close to him, his heat and emotions enveloping her until her pulse kicked up. "It was just a funny choice of words."

"I don't care. The sentiment remains. I'll not have you calling me a liar."

"Then don't lie." Kira shot him a look and pressed herself back against the rocky surface when Brogan's hands shot out to cage her in place.

"I'm not lying." Brogan's eyes drilled into hers. "I don't care what you or anyone in this town thinks of me. I don't have to make friends. I don't have to be well-liked. I don't care if I'm included in parties. But what I do very much care about is my reputation and my character. I will not have you or anyone else calling me a liar."

He was dead serious, Kira realized, as she let out a long slow breath. Even if it wasn't the truth, which she still needed to figure out, at the very least, Brogan believed every word he was saying. The moment drew out between them and Kira realized that Brogan was not going to move or let her out until she said something. Even if his actions were a bit domineering, Kira found the lusty side of herself responding to him as a tug of desire pulled at her.

"Perhaps… perhaps there is a better explanation?" Kira finally offered, and breathed a sigh of relief when Brogan dropped his hands. She had been entirely too close to throwing her arms around his neck and pulling him down for another electrifying kiss.

"I don't know what is going on, and that's the truth of it. I went to visit the development the day after Dylan told me about it. From my records, it does look to be on my land. But I swear to you, I have no part in this. I've contacted the land surveyor to come out and assess where they're building. I couldn't get a straight answer out of any of the men on the crew, and I still don't know the company behind the development. All I can be telling you is that I have had nothing to do with this."

"The development is hurting Fergal's habitat," Kira said. "He told me it's blocking the water from the stream. The other otters are suffering. This is a problem."

"One I'd be more than happy to fix, because I certainly don't want any wildlife to suffer." Brogan spun about and stomped a few feet away, his agitation clear. "I'm an environmental scientist, Kira. Perhaps your limited understanding of this job makes you think I want to destroy the environment?" Brogan whirled again, stomping back to her, clearly working himself up into a snit.

Kira opened her mouth. "I… well…"

"Well, it doesn't, okay? I actually *care* about nature. I care about what gets developed on the land. I study habitats to see how they would be harmed by development. I look at sustainable and environmentally-friendly options for inevitable progress. My whole life is designed around putting nature first. The fact that you would even think…"

Brogan broke off, pressing his lips together, and then let out a stream of low muttered curses.

Kira tried again. "It's just that –"

"It's just that you were willing to believe rumors instead of asking me directly. You... you come out here and kiss me and then turn around and think poorly of me. All of which I had no say in."

Brogan was close to her again and Kira's stomach did a funny little dance as he leaned closer to her. Her eyes hovered on his mouth for a second.

"Yes, that! With those witchy eyes and come-hither mouth. You'll seduce me and condemn me in the same breath."

Kira realized now how truly angry he was, and it was more than just about her assumptions of his involvement in the development. He was genuinely hurt.

"One is separate from the other," Kira said.

"And I have no say in this? You've made up your mind and that's it?"

"It's not that simple."

"Well? How am I wrong then? Tell me." Brogan leaned over her again, and she realized just how much taller he was than her. In other circumstances, she might have felt protected. But right now, all she felt was shame. The man was right. The least she could have done was had the decency of asking him first instead of accusing him.

"You're..." Kira sighed. "You're absolutely right. That's the truth of it. I can be a little hotheaded at times. I should've been asking you directly instead of jumping to conclusions."

"Thank you." Brogan stepped back and forced himself to take a few deep breaths.

"You've a temper on you, then. I wasn't expecting that." Kira watched Brogan carefully, wondering just how to proceed with him. If anything, her attraction for him had grown.

"It doesn't rear its head often. I prefer to live a calm and peaceful life. Anger is a disruptive emotion. Especially in nature." Brogan didn't look at her, but gazed out toward the water instead.

Kira took a moment before coming to a decision. There were two things she realized quickly – that she was very attracted to Brogan, and that she would have no future with him if she hid who she was. Not after he'd reacted so fiercely to the accusation of being a liar. If Kira fancied any sort of… anything with him, she'd need to be upfront from the beginning. A shiver of nerves worked through her as she walked to him and stopped just inches away, looking up at his still-angry face.

"I'm sorry."

"Thank you." The tension in Brogan's brow smoothed.

"Since it's trust you're on about, I suppose I should be straight with you now."

"What about?" A hint of suspicion flitted through Brogan's eyes.

"Well, I can tell if you're being honest, you see. Not just by your words, but in other ways."

"You can read my mind? Like when you talk to Fergal?"

The fact that he so easily accepted her ability to talk to

animals only solidified Kira's decision to be up-front with him.

"Not quite. But I do have other abilities. I can see auras, for one thing. Another ability is a little trickier. I can read people, or items, through touch."

"I... you'll need to explain that a bit more for me before I can be understanding what you're saying."

Kira reminded herself that he was a scientist. "I can't quite say how it works, other than magick. I suppose if you were to study it, there might be some way to maybe discern energy patterns... universal memories... I'm not really sure. But, for example, I could pick up someone's hat or car keys and get flashes of the history behind them. Like where the hat has been, or who owned it. With people, I can touch you and see if you're lying. Or see your memories. That kind of thing."

"That must be handy," Brogan said. "Or annoying. I can't decide."

"It's both." Kira laughed, warmth blooming through her. "So, I'll ask of you – will you allow me to touch you? To read you?"

"What will you see if you do?"

"I don't know. Sometimes, depending on the connection, it can go really deep. I can see your personal history. Your truths, your lies, your vulnerabilities. It's why I'm asking you for permission."

"But you kissed me. Didn't you get all that already then?"

"Good question." Kira appreciated his quick mind. "But I didn't kiss you with the intent to read you, so no, I didn't get anything other than how I felt."

"And how did you feel?" Brogan's eyes met hers and Kira felt her breath slow at the heat she found there.

"I felt lit up," Kira said, her voice soft. "Like I'd been electrified. All my nerves stood on end and did a little dance."

"I wonder if it would be the same. Again."

Kira did too. She leaned in, tilting her lips up to his.

"Wait," Brogan said, stepping back. "If you can read me as you say, then do that first. I don't want you to kiss me again if you have any doubts about my character."

"Are you certain? I may see things you don't want to share."

"I have nothing that I'm ashamed of."

"People say that, but very rarely do they mean it," Kira murmured.

"There may be things that make me sad. But not ashamed."

"I don't have to…"

"No. I insist. If you truly believe this is something you can do and it helps you, then go ahead."

There it was, Kira thought, a subtle challenge thrown down. Brogan would need evidence that her magick was real. She didn't blame him – he was a scientist, after all. Reaching forward, she silently held out her hands. Brogan took her measure before placing his palms in her own. Her first thought was that these were strong hands – used to manual labor, and with a great love for the earth. Closing her eyes, she pulled down her mental shields and allowed the flood of Brogan's thoughts and memories to pour over her.

First, she could immediately see he was telling the

truth of the development on his land. He'd been just as surprised at the discovery as she had been. Happy to know he wasn't willingly destroying the land, Kira smiled. Then it disappeared as she was sucked deeper into his memories, where a sad little boy brought a limp bouquet of flowers to his mother. Kira gasped when a resounding slap sent the boy stumbling back, and she raised a hand to her cheek, breaking contact.

"Find what you're looking for?" Brogan asked, his face devoid of emotion.

"I did. You were as equally surprised about the development as I was," Kira said.

"But that's not what made you gasp and put a hand to your cheek, is it?" Brogan pressed his lips together and looked out over her shoulder. "Tell me what you saw and I can confirm if it's true."

"Oh, Brogan. We don't have to do this," Kira whispered.

"Yes, we do. If you're willing to be vulnerable with me and show me your powers, or whatever you call them, then I have to be vulnerable back."

It shocked Kira that he would see it that way and not as an intrusion of his privacy. That he had the emotional depth to understand her vulnerability and was open to sharing himself with her was touching.

"I saw you as a young boy. Bringing flowers to your mother, I believe. She… rejected them," Kira said.

"She hit me. She often did. It wasn't all that hard or painful. It was just her way of expressing her dissatisfaction with life."

"I'm so sorry, Brogan."

"I've come to terms with it."

Kira highly doubted that. Could anyone ever get over that kind of rejection from their parents?

"Nevertheless, I'm sorry for your pain."

"At least I had Gran. She was a balm for my soul."

"You loved her."

"Very much, yes." Brogan sighed and ran a hand over his face. "So it seems you've got some extra-sensory abilities. I'm not sure what to make of them, but the science side of me would love to figure out how it all works."

"I'm not surprised. I might humor you there." Kira smiled up at him. "I wouldn't mind knowing how it works either."

"You're… really something, Kira. I think about you…" Brogan brought a hand up to brush against her cheek before entwining a lock of her hair around his finger.

"I think about you too, Brogan."

He tugged her hair gently, pulling her closer. Then he bent forward, his lips brushing hers in the sweetest of kisses. There it was again, Kira thought as she leaned into the kiss, not wanting the contact to break. A current of energy pulsed through her at his touch. It energized her, seeming to light her up and heat her from the inside, and she wanted more of it. Kira blinked up at Brogan as he broke the kiss, feeling drugged with her need for him.

"I felt it too," Brogan whispered. "The electricity. You're right, Kira."

"About what?"

"You're magick."

CHAPTER 11

*K*ira bowed over him, her hair curtaining around his face, closing Brogan in as if they were in their own secret world together. He traced his hands up her sides, reveling in the soft skin he found there, sighing as he found the smooth slope of her breast. Kira moaned softly in pleasure as his hand teased her nipple. The bud pebbled under his hand, her sigh echoing her desire. When he slid inside her, she sheathed him tightly, and Brogan let out his own moan of desire as the electric current he had felt from their kiss earlier that day flooded through him.

Brogan blinked awake, a sheen of sweat across his chest, and stared at the dim light of his alarm clock. Five in the morning was a fine time for an erotic dream, and he groaned, banging his head back into the pillow and covering his eyes with his arm.

He wanted her, there was no doubt about that.

Brogan thought back to their kiss earlier that day. She'd unnerved him when she'd been able to see into his past. He wondered why that particular memory had surfaced for her, but if anything, it very neatly summed up his past for her. He was just grateful that she hadn't happened on any of his past relationships.

He relished the memory of their kiss. It was as though he could still feel it – her lips on his, the current of energy buzzing between them, like two magnets snapping together.

It was like no kiss he'd ever had before in his life.

He didn't have the best track record with women, and that was the truth of it. Brogan had never mastered the finesse his mates had with picking up women. Instead, he'd fallen fast for pretty much any woman who had shown an interest in him, and his mates were endlessly grilling him about ignoring very obvious red flags. A hope-less romantic, he always ignored his friends' advice until inevitably it all came crashing down around him. The problem was, Brogan always wanted to believe the good in everyone. He never believed that a woman would use him for his money or just because she was lonely, or – in one notable instance – to make her ex-boyfriend jealous. If a woman was sweet to him, Brogan would take her at her word and find himself falling.

It was why he'd sworn off dating for the last few years. Brogan had decided he couldn't trust his own heart, and therefore, until he figured out his own issues, it was best not to enter the dating pool. Those waters were just too dangerous for him. After a few years without dating, as well as some deep introspection, Brogan had finally come to the conclusion that one of the reasons he so desperately wanted to fall in love was that he was trying to fulfill the deep-rooted need to be loved – affection that he hadn't received from his parents growing up. After his revelation at the pub about wanting a family, Brogan had come to understand that what he had been searching for all along was love to fill his home.

Because *he* had love to give.

Brogan knew he was a good person, and he was determined that he could be a great partner to the right woman. It just seemed that the ones he chose – or the ones who chose him – were like oil to his water. His picker was off, as his mates would say.

And now, after all this time on his own, Kira had blindsided him in the gallery the day he'd gone to look for some art for a blank wall in the cottage. He'd actually seen a piece he loved, but he'd been so agitated after talking to Kira that he'd clammed up and had left quickly with only a few postcards. That was another thing that hampered him – at times, he could be quite shy. Brogan was in his element in nature and in the quiet. His brain couldn't seem to deliver casual banter if he was bewitched by a lovely woman.

And Kira had certainly bewitched him.

She likely *was* a witch, he realized, and took his arm off his eyes to blink at the ceiling. And wasn't that just something? Him, a scientist, entranced by a beautiful woman who could talk to animals and conjure up memories from the deepest recesses of his brain. The question remained – could he handle this? Would he be comfortable trying to date someone like her?

Remnants of his dream slid over him and Brogan shifted, wrapping his arms around the pillow next to him.

He pictured Kira lying next to him, blinking awake with a tangle of curls haloing her head.

It felt right.

It made no sense, his instant attraction to her, nor the abilities she had. But Brogan would be lying to himself if he said he wasn't already hooked. The question was – what could he do about it?

Doing what he always did when he had a problem to mull over, Brogan dressed quickly and made a cup of tea to take outside. He sat at a little bench in front of the cottage, his back leaning against the smooth stone walls surrounding the garden, and took a sip of his tea as the sun crested the horizon.

"She's worth it, you know."

Brogan swore as he sloshed hot tea on his lap. He jumped up, whirling to look around him. A woman, glowing faintly in the wan morning light and partially transparent, stood by his cottage.

"Sure and I'm losing my mind…" Brogan decided, frozen in place as the woman moved – no, *floated* – closer.

The woman stopped near him, studying his face. "You look like her."

"Like whom?"

"Ah, I'm sorry. I shouldn't speak of two different women at the same time. You've the look of your gran. She was a friend of mine."

"Fiona," Brogan determined.

"You're correct. Go on, sit back down; you're shaking like a leaf in a cold autumn wind."

"I'll admit, you've surprised me."

"I suppose. I should know better than to be sneaking up on people, but it gives me a laugh."

"I can see why Gran liked you."

"We had a similar sense of humor." A faint smile flitted across Fiona's face.

"Is she well?"

"Aye, she's well. She's been good company to me on the other side. Her magick isn't strong enough to come over, but she sends her love."

"She does?" Warmth flooded through Brogan, and even if he was dreaming this episode, it felt nice to hear that Gran was okay.

"She does. She says not to worry about the land development. You'll get it sorted soon enough. Oh, and that she likes Kira for you. Not like that Eloise lass you dated."

"I hardly dated... Eloise thought I had more money than I..." Brogan shook his head and pinched his nose. Was he really out here arguing with a ghost at sunrise?

"Kira's of my blood. She's a good woman."

"I don't doubt it. She's enchanting." Brogan shifted, uncomfortable about discussing his love life with a ghost. Frankly, having *any* conversation with a ghost was unsettling.

"She is. She can be reckless, impulsive, and hotheaded. But she's loyal to the core, and a better friend you'll never find. She's worth your time."

"I was just sitting out here thinking about her, actually. Trying to wrap my head around her... magick, is it? Powers?"

"Ah, she told you already? Isn't that nice? That's a gift in itself, you know."

"How so?"

"There's many of us with extra abilities. Some have been persecuted through the years. Witch hunts, banned by the Church, that kind of thing. It's made it so that those of us who have such powers think twice before sharing that. She must trust you."

"She thought I was destroying the land."

"You obviously convinced her otherwise, or she wouldn't have shown herself to you. It takes courage to do that... especially when you don't know how the other person will react. You wouldn't have been the first person in her life to curse her out or run from her."

"I kissed her."

"A much better response, in my humble opinion."

Brogan laughed and stretched his legs out in front of him.

"I was sitting out here trying to figure out what to do next. I have a tendency to ignore warning signs in relationships. And a woman having magickal powers could be viewed by some as a big red flag."

"Is that how you feel?"

"Oddly enough, despite my very scientific background, no."

"Science and the pursuit of understanding the natural world is surprisingly well-linked with the magickal energies of the universe."

"Is it? I suppose. At the end of the day, we're all in the pursuit of knowledge."

"So, what will it be then? Will you run from her or stay?"

"Stay."

"Good. But... well, she'll hate me for saying this, but take it slow with her. She's fallen too fast in the past. She needs to learn what it's like when a man woos her. Respects her. Take it slowly and get to know her."

"I can understand that. I've fallen too fast before, too. I was thinking I would ask her on a hike. She likes nature as well, which I approve of. I was thinking we could talk more. I... well, it may be silly, but I think I have an idea."

"Tell me."

Twenty minutes later, Fiona had disappeared as quickly as she'd arrived and Brogan would've been hard-pressed to explain the moment to anyone. But he felt good, he realized, as though he'd had a breakfast talk with his very own gran. If anything, the conversation had helped him come to a decision. Picking up his phone, he sent Kira a text message; he didn't want to wake her this early.

But he did want her first thought of the morning to be of him.

CHAPTER 12

*H*e'd asked her on a *walk*.

Kira hummed as she rearranged a corner of the gallery featuring some lovely moody watercolors by a young local artist. It had been a week since her parents had departed for Portugal, and Kira found she was really enjoying managing the gallery along with Morgan. The pace was much busier than she had anticipated, and she was meeting people from all over the world who wandered into the shop looking for a little piece of Ireland to take home with them.

She had the gallery to herself for the rest of the week, as Morgan was traveling to Dublin to oversee a new exhibit. Kira had been busy all day fulfilling online orders or chatting with customers, but she found she didn't mind it. As a photographer, it wasn't uncommon for her to be on her feet most of the day anyway, and keeping busy meant that Kira didn't have too much time to obsess over Brogan's text from earlier this morning.

It had been the first thing she'd read when she'd awakened after a fitful night of sleep. The kiss they'd shared yesterday had stayed in her mind all night, along with the certainty that once he'd had a moment away from her to process what had happened between them, Brogan would be scared off by her ability to read him. He wouldn't be the first to be put off by her abilities, that was the truth of it; it was something Kira had grown to accept even if she didn't like it. Her mother had always told her to be patient – that the right man would see her for who she was through and through, and would love her because of it, not despite it. So far, she'd yet to have that experience, but she held out hope.

Seeing Brogan's text this morning had filled her with such joy that she'd been all but singing all day. With one simple request – to go on a walk – he'd kicked her insecurities aside and opened the door to a hope that maybe they could have something more.

Granted, she'd been a little surprised about his choice of activities – he wasn't expressly asking her on a date. But he also wasn't running away screaming, so she was willing to give it a chance. Plus, she loved going for long walks, so it wasn't exactly like he'd invited her for an unpleasant activity. It was just the waiting that would drive her crazy, she decided – it would be two days yet before she'd have time for an afternoon wander over the hills as she'd agreed to.

"Well, now, who's out wool-gathering?" Gracie demanded, her hands on her hips as she stood in front of Kira.

"Oh my – Gracie! I didn't even see you there."

"Clearly. The place could've been burning down around you, and you'd never have known it!"

"I'm sorry. I'm distracted."

"I can see that. I've brought you some more of my candles; the stock was getting low."

"Ah, brilliant. We sold the last one yesterday. They really are wonderful, Gracie. All of your products are."

"I know." Gracie smiled and began to unpack the box she'd put on the gallery's counter. "But do go on."

"You're amazing. A goddess. A model of a woman." Kira laughed as Gracie pirouetted and did a little curtsy.

"Thank you. Feel free to remind Dylan of that any time."

"Why would I need to? He's besotted with you."

"He is, isn't he? I do love my man."

"As you should. You've landed a good one."

"And speaking of… is that handsome neighbor of mine the reason you're so distracted today?"

"He is, at that," Kira admitted, opening one of Gracie's candles and sniffing it. "Yum. What's this one made of?"

"Juniper and sea salt."

"It's lovely. I'm taking this for my room."

"You can have it if you dish on Brogan."

"It's a deal. I confronted him about the development. He got really upset with me for thinking he was a liar."

"Men will do that."

"But he wasn't lying. He let me read him. He truly didn't know anything about the development and is just as upset about it as we are."

"Wait…" Gracie looked up from where she was stacking the candles on a row of shelves along the wall. "A couple things there. He didn't know about the development?"

"No. And he isn't getting straight answers on who's heading up the project."

"I'll get Dylan on it. That man can find out anything."

"Liam, too. The both of them could be in the mob."

"That's the truth of it, though I'd never be telling them that. They'd take it as a compliment."

"They would at that."

"Secondly, he let you read him? How'd that go down?"

"Oh – well…" Kira trailed off as she thought back to what she'd learned and how he'd responded. "He was willing to be vulnerable with me. And instead of closing himself off to me when I pulled out some sensitive information, he kissed me."

"Did he now?" A smile bloomed on Gracie's face. "And what was this sensitive information?"

"I'd rather not say. Let's just leave it at he's had a troubled childhood. I would feel bad sharing."

Instantly contrite, Gracie moved to Kira's side.

"Of course – I shouldn't have asked. That kind of stuff isn't for gossip, is it now?"

"No."

"But the kiss is. Give me every last detail."

"It lit me up inside. That's twice now." Kira sighed and hugged her arms around herself. "It felt good. In a way that I haven't felt before."

"How'd you leave it?"

"We said our goodbyes. I didn't want to press him on spending time together because I was certain he'd go home and be convinced I was a nutter after he thought about my magick."

"And? Have you heard from him?"

"He texted me first thing this morning and asked me to go for a walk."

"A walk?" Gracie frowned as she thought about it.

"Unusual, yes. But I like going for walks."

"He's good for you. This is good. I like that he didn't run away. This is all good stuff, Kira."

"I like it too. It was nice that I wasn't left wondering if he thought I was crazy or something."

"And even if it's just friendly, I mean, no harm done, right?"

"That's true. Though I'm kind of hoping for more. But even if he wants to just be friends, at least he's being forward with it. I can appreciate that."

"Maybe walk him past the cove. You'll know what you're dealing with pretty quickly then."

"You think? I don't know…" Kira thought about the stories of how the cove would glow in the presence of true love. Gracie and Fi swore by it, but she'd yet to see anything magickal from the waters of the cove. Oh, she could feel the magick there – it was almost tangible, as if she could reach out and touch it. But she'd never visibly seen anything.

"Just a thought." Gracie smiled.

"I hate when you do this," Kira grumbled.

"I didn't say you *had* to go to the cove."

"No, but now the thought is there. And it's all I'll be thinking about."

"Do what you wish."

"You're a pain in the arse, Gracie."

"You love me."

"Maybe. Only if you give me another candle."

"It's yours. Get the cedar vanilla one. It's good for seduction."

Kira laughed, but took her advice. It certainly couldn't hurt.

CHAPTER 13

*K*ira couldn't think of the last time she had put so much thought into her appearance for going on a walk. Normally, she just peeked out the window, gauged the weather, and pulled on whatever outer layers she would need. But she'd be lying to herself if she said she didn't care what Brogan thought of her looks. Perhaps it was a bit vain, but she'd made her career out of photographing people, and the image people presented mattered.

Today she wanted to appear fresh-faced and happy to be going on a hike with Brogan, so she chose a deep mauve jumper and a heathered knit cap, and pulled her hair into two loose braids on either side of her face. She threaded dangly turquoise earrings through her ears and wrapped a bright red scarf around her neck. Pausing a moment longer than usual, Kira studied her face in the mirror. She looked excited… and dare she say hopeful? It had been a while since spending time with someone had elicited such a response in her.

A half-hour later, Kira pulled her car to a stop along the cliff road that would lead them toward the cove. She'd taken a day to mull over Gracie's suggestion of walking near there, and then had decided – why not? The worst that could happen was that she wouldn't see the magickal blue glowing light. That would mean Brogan wasn't her forever after – but he could still be a perfect candidate for Mr. Right Now. Kira had to keep reminding herself that she wasn't moving back to Grace's Cove, so she shouldn't be thinking long-term anyway. Live in the moment, Kira told herself. She'd been operating that way for so long, it was odd that she wasn't defaulting to that mode now.

Fergal's otter page was doing fantastically, much to Kira's amusement. The page was building momentum for support in protecting the otter habitats, and people around Ireland were falling in love with the otter and all his cute mannerisms. It would only be a matter of time before Kira could formally submit a petition, and she was certain she'd be able to make a difference in helping to preserve Fergal's habitat. After she'd seen to that, and once her mother came home to run the gallery again, there would be nothing to keep Kira in Grace's Cove. Already she'd been fielding inquiries for her services, and there were a few notable offers that had piqued her interest.

"You look lovely," Brogan commented immediately when she stepped from her car. "Like a wildflower just sprung up after a spring rain."

Charmed, Kira twinkled up at Brogan, trying to remember the last time someone had paid her such a compliment. "That's a fine compliment indeed. And you're looking very handsome yourself, so you are," Kira said.

"Well, thank you. Now that we've determined we're a smart-looking pair on this sunshiny afternoon, shall we promenade?" Brogan affected an aristocratic accent and executed a stiff bow for Kira.

"Indeed, good sir, I do believe we shall," Kira laughed and stepped next to him. She refrained from reaching for his hand, as she wasn't sure what kind of walk this was, and instead fell neatly into step with him as they began to follow the lightly worn path that hugged the cliff line leading toward the cove. If Kira knew anything about Gracie, it was that she was all but hanging out the window of her cottage at the moment, trying to spy on them with binoculars. A joyful bark reached her, confirming her suspicions.

"Does someone have a dog nearby?" Brogan asked.

"That's Rosie. Grace and Dylan's dog. Her cottage isn't far from here. See? You can just see it up the way." Kira pointed across the hill.

"Oh, you're right. I think I got a little turned around when I came down here. Is Rosie friendly?" Brogan asked as the dog raced at breakneck speed across the field toward them.

"Aye, she's a boisterous one, but as loving as can be. Hey there, Miss Rosie. Are you joining us on a walk then?" Kira crouched and scratched behind Rosie's soft ears. The dog smiled at her and then turned her head, her tongue lolling out as she looked up at Brogan.

Friend? Food?

"She wants to know if you're a friend and if you have food," Kira said.

"I am a friend, Rosie. Nice to meet you." Brogan grinned as he bent over and petted Rosie. "As to food, I don't think I have anything that's dog-friendly. And I don't want to get in trouble with Grace for making her dog sick."

"Sorry, Rosie. You'll have to beg your treats from someone else then."

Let's run! Running is fun!

Kira laughed as Rosie took off sprinting in circles around them. The dog was clearly as delighted with the soft spring day as Kira was. A gentle breeze brought the scents of damp and earth, along with a touch of the sea, and Kira tilted her face up to the sun for a moment.

"It's nice to have a clear day, isn't it?"

"It is. I was beginning to think the rain would never lift," Brogan agreed.

They continued their walk along the cliff's edge. Far below them, the waves crashed against the rocks, and gulls swooped lazily in the air.

"I rarely tire of the rain, I'll admit," said Kira. "I do love the moody lighting. It provides such a nice backdrop for portraits."

"How did you get into photography? Was it something your Mam encouraged you to do?" Brogan picked up a stick and waited for Rosie to turn around before tossing it across the field. Rosie, delighted at the chance for play, raced after it.

"Not necessarily photography. My mother encouraged creativity in general. But she was often distracted or absorbed in her own work, so she'd set me in the corner with a pot of paint or colored pencils and leave me to it."

"How old were you? That sounds like it could cause quite a mess."

"Aye, I did. But she never yelled at me for that. So long as I was expressing myself, Mam was fine with what I created. My da struggled with it for a while before finally giving up and agreeing that so long as I was in the studio, I could make any mess of it I'd like."

"And how did that lead to a camera?"

"Well," Kira said, slanting a look up at Brogan, "it has to do with my abilities, really."

"I'm listening." Brogan gave her a small smile of encouragement.

"I would draw people – stick figures, really – when I was younger, and they were always surrounded in bubbles of color. It was there my Mam picked up on my ability to see auras. One day she had left a camera in the studio and young me thought maybe the camera would catch the auras I could see. I wasn't entirely aware at the time that I was seeing something most others can't. Imagine my disappointment when the film came back with no colors around people."

"I can imagine."

"But something else was born of that disappointment. Instead of letting me wallow in a temper, my Mam sat down with me and we went through each photo. She talked to me about angles and lighting. We compared the moods of each photo and discussed how different ones told a different story. I was transfixed. It was the first time something had really gotten its hooks into me instead of me just playing with a pot of paint."

"How old were you?"

"I was nine. I kept asking my Mam to use the camera, and soon they realized how serious I was about learning about photography. My father brought heaps of books home from the library for me, and for Christmas that year I had my first camera of my own. While the rest of the girls at school were playing with dolls, I was off tromping through the fields taking photos of bugs and flowers."

"I can relate to that. I didn't really fit in with the other kids either."

"I wouldn't say I 'didn't fit in' so much as I just chose to follow what excited me. I had friends, and I was – well, *am* – lucky to have wonderful parents who support me in my career."

"You didn't bring your camera today?"

"Of course I did." Kira laughed and patted her pack. "It's pretty much always with me."

"Ah. I like watching you with the camera. Very focused. I can see why you don't mind wandering solo through the hills. Your face lights up when you're working."

"I suspect your solo trips through the hills were a little different growing up?" Kira broached the subject gently, not wanting him to feel uncomfortable discussing what she'd seen the other day. "Where did you grow up?"

"Outside Kinsale. A beautiful area, truly."

"Aye, Kinsale's lovely."

"But no, my excursions into the wilderness were much

more based on escapism than any driving passion. Though I must say, if it wasn't for that time in my life, I'm not certain I would have found this career, and it's brought me joy."

"A blessing it is, then. Tough times have a way of defining an individual. There are many paths you could've taken. You chose one that seeks to protect what was your safe space."

"I... I guess I never looked at it like that before." Brogan stopped for a moment and then shook his head with a little laugh. "You're right, though. Nature was my safe space. Home was not."

"I'm sorry for that. And you didn't fit in at school either?"

"I had a few good friends. I'm naturally a quieter sort. Combine shyness with a home that wasn't good to bring friends to, and I had a fairly lonesome childhood."

Her heart hurt for the little boy in Brogan. She could see them both, wandering the hills in their youth: her in excitement and passion, chattering away with the animals; him seeking solace and safety. Two children – different sides of the same coin.

"And now?"

"Now, well, I'm content. Those same friends grew into life-long ones. I met a few more along the way in university." Brogan laughed again. "I can't say that my fellow scientists and I were the most extroverted bunch, but I'd found my people."

"And your family?"

"It's just me now." Brogan shrugged, though there was an ache to his voice that caught at Kira's heartstrings.

"Gran was the hardest to lose. She acted as a de facto mother to me, I suppose."

"She's still here. Not that it's all that much comfort, I suppose. It's hard to lose people. But I can tell you that, with my abilities, I'm sometimes able to see those who have crossed over. Your loved ones are near, even if it seems they are lost to you."

"So I've learned," Brogan mumbled. "Either way, I really try to focus on the memories. I like thinking about our times together or the lessons she imparted to me. I feel like sometimes the best way to keep people alive is to just talk about them or think about them. Then the essence of them isn't really lost, is it?"

"I agree. Would you like to tell me about her? Your gran?"

"I will. Someday. But I can tell you she would've loved you. The two of you would have a whole house built for the otters by now." Brogan smiled.

"Ah, a woman after my own heart then."

"Speaking of the otters, shall we find a spot to sit? I have something I want to talk to you about."

"There's a picnic table a ways further, by the cove. Dylan put it in after he moved in with Gracie. He doesn't like to go into the cove so much, but loves to sit and look out over the water. Plus, I think he was hoping to deter others from the long climb down into the cove, and to keep them in safety at the top."

"Is this the infamous cove? The one my gran always warned me to stay away from?"

"Indeed it is. Did you stay away from it?"

"I was a risk-averse child, I'll admit. And because

Gran was the only adult in my life who had stood for me, I always respected her wishes."

"I'd tease you for not being some badass rebel, but that's just sweet enough to make me want to hug you, Brogan."

"I'll take a hug. It's been a while." Brogan stopped so suddenly that Kira ran into his back. She'd fallen into line behind him on the part of the path that narrowed near the entrance to the cove.

"Whoops, sorry for that…" Kira trailed off as he turned and put his arms around her. Automatically, she wrapped her arms around his waist. Uncertain of what this meant, or what he might be thinking, Kira pressed her cheek to his chest instead of tilting her head up to look at him and inviting his kiss. The moment drew out as they stood there, a lovely energy pulsing between them, before Brogan cleared his throat and stepped back.

"Thanks. I think I needed that," Brogan said, his voice cheerful as he continued toward the picnic table, which was now in sight.

Kira hummed a little note in her throat. The hug had woken up all her senses, and now she felt more confused than ever as she followed Brogan to the table, where he'd already begun to unpack his backpack.

"A picnic?"

"Sadly, not a proper one. I was busy with other things, so I just grabbed a few nibbles. Will a thermos of tea and a few scones suit?"

"Aye, that's lovely. Thanks for thinking of it," Kira said.

She swung her foot over the bench and absentmindedly

reached out to stroke Rosie's ears. The dog had come forward to lay her head on the bench, her eyes on the food laid out on the table.

"You're not starving. I know for a fact that Gracie feeds you."

Food.

"Not dog food."

Fine. Rosie settled into the grass beneath the table, just in case any scraps were to fall.

"I feel bad now. I wish I had something for her."

"I can promise you, she is very well-fed. And an expert at begging."

"In that case, I will push my guilt aside and enjoy my scone."

Kira smiled at him across the table, taking a sip of the tea he had poured for her, content to sit quietly with him. It was nice, she thought, that he didn't feel the need to fill every moment with chatter. They sat in companionable silence for a few moments, watching the ocean, before she finally turned to him.

"Your eyes match the water."

"Do they? They often change," Brogan said. He reached into his bag and pulled out a notebook and a pen.

"Mine do as well. I think with my mood."

"I think of you as a witchy-eyed woman."

Kira slanted her eyes to look at him. "Is that a compliment?"

"Yes. Because I believe that witches can enchant, and I find your eyes very enchanting. Intoxicating, even."

"Oh," Kira breathed, pausing with the scone halfway to her mouth.

"I particularly like how they look after we've kissed. Dreamy and a little clouded. Like a storm is swirling about inside."

"Oh... my." Kira put the scone back down and fanned her face. "I'd say you've worked on your shyness, Brogan."

"It's still a battle, but I think I've come a ways." Brogan grinned and opened his notebook. "Now, to talk to you about what I've brought you here for."

"Ohhh, to have your way with me?" Kira teased, testing him.

The flash of heat in his eyes made a similar response pool deep inside of her, and she wondered what he would do if she launched herself across the table into his lap. The urge was so strong that she forced herself to pick up her scone instead, and pulled it in half.

"This would be for a more business-related matter," Brogan said, the stiffness of his voice belied by the passion in his eyes.

It was an interesting contrast, Kira thought, and wondered what it would take to make him lose control.

"By all means, then." Kira swept her arm out. "Do proceed."

"It has come to my attention that you and I share a like-minded goal."

"Is that so? Which goal is this?" Please say sex, please say sex, Kira thought.

"Well, the goal of stopping the development. And protecting the otters' habitat." Brogan cleared his throat as Kira looked at him blankly for a moment. "Was that not your intention? I thought you said Fergal needed our help."

"Oh, the otters. Right, right. Yes, I've already started working on that. But I had hoped you'd be giving me some information about the developers as well."

"Well, they're cagey. But I think I'll be able to get a court order to stop their building, as part of the development encroaches on my land. Not all of it, though, so it's a bit tricky. However, I also wanted to look at which part of their development is directly impacting Fergal's habitat. Which led me down another path... and, well..." Brogan took a deep breath before rushing the rest of his words out. "Would you be interested in opening a conservation group with me?"

"Opening a group?" Kira asked.

"Yes. I've been thinking that there seems to be no local conservation group that works to protect this land. In general, it seems the locals look out for it, but I'm meaning to put something more formal in place. Maybe a nature center – trails, education, that kind of thing. Where we'd have legal and formal protection. Are you interested?"

Was she? Kira paused for a moment as she mulled it over. It sounded like a lot of work, and something which would require her time to be spent in Grace's Cove, rooted in one spot. That being said, she did love nature and she knew most of her friends and family would certainly support such a cause. Between the new community center Dylan was building and a nature center, there would be loads of new activities for the locals to participate in. Plus, she'd have the benefit of seeing Fergal happily settled in his protected pond.

"I think there are a lot of positives to this idea of yours. But I have some questions."

"Go for it."

"What about your job? Would you make this your new full-time gig? Or would you be planning to hand off the management to someone else?"

"I'm not rightly sure yet. I've been thinking about – well, a life change of sorts lately. Not that I don't love what I do, but I've been feeling a bit adrift. A part of me thinks this would be a lovely way to honor Gran, her beautiful land, and to contribute to future generations' enjoyment of nature."

"All very noble. But what happens when you've been stuck here for a year with no place to go?"

Brogan laughed at her. "I'll take a holiday then."

"And who will run things while you're gone?"

"Hopefully, a capable manager."

"And how do you plan to be paying for them?"

"With the money that I put into starting this up."

"And once that money runs dry?"

"We solicit donations and offer yearly memberships?" Brogan shook his head at her.

"And if that's not enough to keep it afloat?"

"Then we figure out a way. It's not a multi-million dollar operation, Kira. I think we could run this on a fairly lean budget and still make a difference."

"You say 'we.' But how do you see me involved?"

"I suppose that would be for you to decide. Off the top of my head, I was thinking that with your photography and creative skills, you could be a real asset in raising awareness of what the area provides in the way of plant and animal life, and perhaps work the social media angle to build a following of donors. I was also thinking maybe

you'd like to lead classes for budding nature photographers. Birders and so on..." Brogan trailed off as her
mouth dropped open. "What?"

"You want me to teach photography?"

"I mean... you don't have to. I thought we were just
brainstorming, weren't we?"

"I've never thought about teaching before," Kira
mused. She turned from Brogan, propping her feet up on
the bench, and looked out to the water. The idea of
teaching photography felt... well... she had thought it
would feel silly, but for some reason, it bloomed warm
inside of her. Maybe she'd love it, Kira thought.

"It's just an idea. Something I was kicking about. In
general, what are your thoughts?" Brogan stood and
moved around the side of the table so he could sit next to
her. Kira turned her gaze from the water to his.

"Brogan, I think it's brilliant. Why *shouldn't* you do
something like this? Of course, we need a defined conservation effort here. And I'm sure it'll be welcomed by
everyone in town."

"So you'll help? I'm horrible with photos. I can barely
take a selfie." Brogan shrugged.

"I'll help. In fact, I've already started. Look." Kira
pulled out her phone and brought up her otter Instagram
page.

"In Otter News." Brogan laughed as he scrolled
through her pictures. Turning, he bent his face close to
hers. "I think you're amazing, Kira."

"Thank you. That's sweet of you."

Before she could say anything else, Brogan pressed his
lips to hers in the softest of kisses. He pulled away so

quickly that, had Kira not felt the pulse of energy rush through, her entire body going on full alert, she might have thought she'd imagined it.

"Shall we pack up before it gets dark? I'd love to start outlining some more ideas."

The quick switch of subjects startled Kira – her brain was still fuzzy from his kiss. "Right, yes. Best to get on with it."

Brogan stood and began packing things away, his back to the cove. Kira took a deep breath and turned to the water, forcing her nerves to steady.

When the water of the cove lit from within, Kira's heart twisted.

"Are you coming, then?" Brogan asked.

"Oh, I'm just wool-gathering. So many things to think about. What an exciting idea, Brogan. Thank you for including me!" Kira said, her tone cheerful even though her thoughts were whirling like crazy.

"Of course. I'm looking forward to our partnership."

At that, Kira stared after him as he trotted down the path, Rosie at his side, casual as could be. The man was infuriating! What did he mean by partnership? Were they dating or working together? He'd kissed her, hadn't he? The cove certainly seemed to like him.

Kira needed answers.

CHAPTER 14

"*I*'m so confused."

"Tell me everything. Did you have to be walking where I couldn't see you both?"

"Yes, because you'd already sent Rosie to spy on us."

"Alas, dearest Rosie can't give me the same run-down on the gossip that you can."

"Bothers you, doesn't it?" Kira stuck out her tongue at Gracie. Instead of going home after their walk, she'd stopped by Grace's cottage to do what women everywhere did when they had a crush: dissect every moment of the interaction.

"Uh-oh. This sounds like it's going to turn into a discussion that I'm not welcome for," Dylan said. He was washing dishes at the small sink, looking comfortable and relaxed in a tartan shirt and denim pants.

"You can stay. It's not like Gracie won't tell you everything anyway," Kira grumbled.

"Ah, so you've figured out the secrets of married life already, then." Dylan shot her a grin over his shoulder.

"Sure and I understand you're a package deal now."

"If you really had something you didn't want me to say to Dylan, I would honor that." Grace reached across the table and squeezed Kira's hand. "You know that, right?"

"I do. But you're family, and now so is he. And it's not like I have massive secrets to keep anyway." Kira sighed wistfully. It wasn't that she sought out drama, but every once in a while, it was fun for a little excitement.

"This is about Brogan, I'm taking a guess?" Dylan asked. He'd turned and leaned against the counter, his arms crossed over his chest.

"That is correct. You've met him, Gracie said."

"I have. Initially, I was concerned that he was involved with this secretive development that's happening up the way. I'd like to meet him again without that coloring my impression."

"He could use your help," Kira said.

"How so?"

"He's struggling to find out who's backing this project. It appears there are many layers."

"I like layers." Dylan steepled his fingers in front of him, a wolfish grin on his face. "Let me at them."

"Please do. He's having a surveyor out to double-check that they are, indeed, on the land his gran left to him. If so, I believe he wants to secure a court order to stop development."

"He's speaking my language. I'll look into this imme-diately." Dylan bent and pressed a kiss to Gracie's fore-head before grabbing his laptop from the table, disappearing into their bedroom, and closing the door behind him.

"That's him occupied for the next few hours. He does love a puzzle. And a power-play." Grace wrinkled her nose.

"Like you don't? Your arguments are infamous at this point."

"Aye, I do like going into battle, now don't I?"

"Well, keep that warrior spirit alive; we may have a battle on our hands. The development is disrupting the river that feeds the pond, and you know I'm worried for Fergal."

"Poor thing. We'll help him."

"That's the plan. I'm hoping there are more. I feel like he's lonely. I'm pretty sure otters are social creatures."

"We'll get after it. I could work on a few disruption spells…" Gracie tapped her finger against her lip.

"And that worked out so well for you last time? You were sick for days, you told me."

"Aye. And it was still worth it." Grace raised her voice in case Dylan was listening.

Kira repeated the phrase that had been passed down between Wise Women for generations: "First, do no harm."

"People would think we're nutters. Sitting here discussing talking otters and spells to disrupt construction progress."

"It's not a dull life we live," Kira said.

"It's not – though you seem to think so, with your gallivanting all over the globe. This is the best place on earth, and you know it."

"There's nothing wrong with wanting something different," Kira chided.

Instantly contrite, Gracie reached out and patted Kira's hand again. "You're absolutely right. I'm just saying that because I've enjoyed having you here again."

"Well, I may be here more often if Brogan's idea comes to fruition."

"Tell me," Gracie demanded.

"He wants to start a conservation group. Maybe even build a nature center. His gran left him quite a bit of land and he wants to see it protected, but he's also thinking there could be environmental advocacy, hiking trails, classes... that kind of thing."

"That's a grand idea. And it could go hand-in-hand with Dylan's community center. Oh, he'll love this."

"Brogan asked if I would start it with him. Like do the photos, social media, teach photography classes... the works."

"Is that right?" Gracie leaned back from the table and studied Kira. "How does that make you feel?"

"Um, it feels good. Meaningful. I can see so many opportunities for it to be impactful. And it would be fun to focus more on nature photography instead of celebrities and their big egos."

"And you'd be working closely with Brogan."

"Which at the moment seems a plus." Kira worried her lower lip. "I'm just so confused!"

"Why? You like him."

"He kissed me."

Gracie's eyes lit with excitement. "Just now? On the walk? Oh! Tell me everything."

"It was the smallest of kisses. And yet I had to restrain myself from tackling him to the ground and having my way with him. His kiss just… warms my soul."

Gracie sighed and fanned her face.

"And then he had the nerve to just neatly switch back to talking business. Like nothing had happened at all."

"He did not."

"He did!"

"Interesting," Gracie mused. "Maybe he's just testing the waters. Taking it slow? Or is he shy?"

"Well, he claims he's struggled with shyness his whole life, but I'm not seeing a trace of it." Kira relayed Brogan's sexy compliments to her, which had Gracie mock swooning at the table.

"I'd say he's come a ways from shyness. I like him," Gracie decided. "I think he'll be good for you. You aren't used to this."

"Used to what?"

"A good guy taking his time with you."

"What is that even supposed to mean?"

"Well, think about it," Grace said. She rose, took a plate from the cupboard, and arranged some toffees on it as she spoke. "You travel constantly and you're always one foot out the door. It gives you an expiration date on every relationship you've ever had. It makes it easy to go fast, have fun, and blow a kiss on your way to a new country. You're used to living life at a breakneck pace and your choice in lovers has reflected that. But this?" Grace set the plate on the table between her and Kira, and sat back down. "Well, he's new territory for you."

"I don't know that I like this territory." Kira shoved a piece of toffee into her mouth. The sweetness flooded her senses, but did nothing to detract from the annoyance lancing her stomach.

"That's because you're not in the driver's seat for once. It can be off-putting, I'll admit."

"What can?" Dylan said, coming out of the bedroom with his laptop in hand.

"Not being in control when someone is courting you."

"And you would know this how?" Dylan quirked a smile at Gracie.

"Excuse me, I was very out of control when we were getting together."

"Gracie, I don't think you'd ever let anyone else be in control. You might have lost hold of your temper a few times, but you still took the reins."

"Did I? I don't remember." Gracie laughed.

"I remember my entire crew coming down with mysterious illnesses."

"I didn't mean... That was bad of me." Gracie sighed, a contrite look flashing across her gorgeous face.

"It was. A fine temper you have there, darling."

"Is there something you're needing then? Aside from needling me?"

"Ah, yes. Do you have Brogan's number, Kira? I'd like to speak with him."

"I do." Kira dug in her pack and pulled out her phone to recite the number.

"Brilliant." Dylan disappeared back into the bedroom.

"As I was saying..." Gracie shot a look at the bedroom door. "Why not try to just let this unfold and not put any expectations on it? Enjoy each other's company. See how it goes. What's the rush?"

"See… there's this thing called sex. I quite enjoy it." Kira grabbed another toffee.

"See, there's this thing called sex toys. Have you heard of them?" Gracie parried.

Kira sighed and bent over, banging her forehead lightly against the table.

"It'll be just fine, darling. Let it be. One thing you'll learn about being back in a small town is that the pace is slower, life is unhurried, and things all eventually work out in the end."

"Said like someone who knows she's getting sex tonight."

"Oh, I already had my fill this morning." Gracie beamed brightly at Kira across the table.

"Have I told you how much I hate you?"

CHAPTER 15

*B*y the end of the week, Kira had worked herself into a proper tizzy – though when Morgan mentioned said tizzy, Kira promptly put every effort into appearing cool and collected. Brogan had been in contact through text message and email only, all of which were completely professional and above-board, no matter how much Kira tried to read into them.

"He said he liked my recent otter post on Instagram. Do you think that means something?" Kira asked, scrolling through her phone.

"I'm going to take the phone away from you," Fi said. She'd stopped by the gallery to bring Kira a coffee and have a chat. She'd recently finished up her latest book translation and had been brought up to speed on Kira and Brogan's budding relationship.

"I'm being ridiculous, aren't I?"

"Like a wee schoolgirl who giggles every time her crush walks past," Fi agreed.

Kira narrowed her eyes at Fi and threatened to toss her coffee on her. "I didn't want an honest answer."

"What kind of friend would I be if I was lying to you then?"

"One who cares for my feelings."

Stricken, Fi moved around the counter and wrapped an arm around Kira's shoulders.

"I'm sorry, I am. Are you truly hurting? I thought you were just fussing a bit."

"No." Kira sighed and turned to give Fi a quick hug before stepping back. "It's just that... he's in my mind, you know? And I'm not used to being out of control, I suppose."

"You're not out of control. It's just that this is how things work in relationships that move at a normal pace. It's not something you and I are used to."

"No, it's not. Things are different when you're on the road. Do you miss it then?"

"Long days of travel and many a lonely night on the road? Or finding lovers who mean nothing more to you than a fond memory of a dusty hotel in Morocco?"

"Yes, that," Kira laughed.

"No, I don't. Liam's a large part of that, of course. He anchors me. Plus, we both enjoy traveling together, so we're free to go when we please. But I think I realized I was ready to have a spot of my own again, so long as I knew that I wasn't caged in, if you understand? I finally have a home, but I still know that if I told Liam I needed to go, he'd either figure out a way to go with me or he'd be fine with me traveling off on my own for a bit. I just don't *want* to go without him."

"You like it here then? You don't feel... suffocated? Back home? I know Gracie is fine here, but she's always been fine here. She didn't have the wanderlust we did. She'll die happy as can be in her cottage on the hills with her love."

"That doesn't sound so bad now, does it?"

"No, I suppose not. I just wonder if I could be satisfied staying here."

"Is that what has you in a mood then? You're thinking about staying here longer? Please say yes, please say yes!" Fi did a happy little bounce.

"Aye, it's in the back of my mind, I won't deny it. But I'm worried I'll feel restless."

"I think you're more worried that you'd be giving up the name you've made for yourself."

"There's that as well. I have worked hard to build up my reputation – which would be lost here."

"Now that's just silly. You can live here and be selective about the assignments you take, is all. Sort of like... a VIP photographer. People have to get on a waiting list to have you."

"I feel like I'll end up taking schoolchildren's portraits and photographing birthday parties if I stay here."

"Nothing wrong with that either, is there?"

"No, you're right. But could you imagine? I go from the wilds of Africa or being backstage at a sold-out concert to photographing little Susie smashing cake in her face."

"When you put it that way... I do see where the one would be less appealing than the other. But aren't there other ways to utilize your skills? You certainly have a diverse portfolio. And you're sitting on a goldmine as it is."

"How so?"

"Why aren't you selling your prints? Here, in the galleries? Aislinn has asked you for years. People love your photography. Your work doesn't have to be printed in a magazine article or on the cover of a new album for it to have value, you know."

"Okay, sure and you've a point there. I haven't given it serious thought."

"Perhaps you should. Just look at this beauty here. You're telling me your photos won't hold up?" Fi swept her arm out to the gallery.

Kira walked around the counter and out into the space, studying it with fresh eyes. Rays of sunlight slitted through wide front windows, picking up the honey tones in the worn wood floor. Gallery lighting brought out the moody tones of her mother's paintings, and the driftwood shelves holding Gracie's goods were charming. It was a good space – classy and elegant, while also being warm and inviting. A space that would let a new collector feel welcome and encouraged to invest in art, while also catering to those with a seasoned eye.

"Right here," Kira muttered, coming to a stop on an accent wall that was now empty due to a recent sale. Painted a deep grey – the color of the ocean before the rains unleashed – the space would be a perfect spot to highlight some of Kira's recent landscape shots.

"Exactly. You could do a dreamy field picture, angry waters of the cove, maybe some of the stone circles in the area. A snapshot of our part of Ireland. I believe photographs would sell equally as well as paintings."

"I'm certain they would. Even some black-and-whites would be stunning here." Kira thought about old Mr. Murphy in his newsboy cap, grinning with a pint of Guinness in his hand. "Can you see Mr. Murphy here?"

"Oh, he'd love that. Truly he would. You have to take his photo."

"I believe I will. Thanks, Fi. You've given me a lot to think about. As has Brogan."

"A nature center, huh?"

"It's a grand idea. And he's asked me to do some photography there as well."

"Has he now? Maybe he wants to spend more time with you."

"Who's to say? The man kisses me and then talks business two seconds later."

"When do you see him next?"

"We've a meeting today at Gallagher's to discuss the recent developments."

"Oh?" Fi got straight down to the important stuff. "What will you wear?"

"It doesn't matter. It's business. I think Dylan's coming as well."

Fi laughed. "I repeat: What will you wear?"

"Will this not do?" Kira looked down to her favorite leather pants and boots, which she'd paired with a loose cream blouse.

"This is lovely. The pants and boots are a yes. But… what about something more vibrant up top? To bring out your eye color?"

"I have a heather green top…"

"Go put that on. And a little eyeshadow. Just a hint. Maybe some lip gloss? I'll watch the gallery."

"It's not a date." Kira was already halfway to the door.

"Nevertheless, you can still look appetizing."

"Don't I always?" Kira laughed at Fi's muttered response and clambered up the stairs to change.

She pulled on a scoop-necked top and then stopped in front of her mirror. Her hair was wild around her head, as it usually was, and she tucked a few pins with sparkles on them in the mass of it to add a little pizazz. Picking up her makeup, she lightly shaded her lids with a soft purple that immediately popped the green tones in her eyes. Blowing herself a kiss, she ran back downstairs, her mind already whirling with portrait ideas for the gallery.

"Perfect. You look like the cool girl that everyone wants to hang out with."

"I *am* the cool girl that everyone wants to hang out with," Kira said, then laughed, "Kidding, kidding."

"I was going to say… someone has gotten all high and mighty these days."

"Not even close. I can't even get a date with the nerdy scientist with sexy bedroom eyes."

"Have you really tried?" Fi asked, picking up her purse.

"I suppose I haven't, have I? I've been mooning about waiting on him."

"Might I suggest you make a move then?"

"I think that's a delightful suggestion."

"Good luck. Maybe I need to get some food at

Gallagher's later," Fi mused. "I'm sure Liam would be interested in talking about the nature center."

"Oh sure, then. Why not invite everyone to the meeting? That'll be a fine date, won't it?" Kira glared at her.

"You're the one who said it's not a date," Fi laughed as she ran out the door.

Kira stomped her foot. Lovely, she thought; now the whole town would be sitting in on their meeting later. Sighing, she turned back to the counter and pulled out a notepad. She might as well get some of these ideas out of her head, otherwise she wouldn't be able to focus on her date later.

Meeting, she reminded herself. It was just a meeting.

CHAPTER 16

*H*e looked good. As in, *really* good, Kira thought, her stomach doing a nervous little dance when she walked through the doors of Gallagher's and saw him already seated at a corner booth. He wore a plaid shirt in hues of green and black, with a light grey thermal beneath. Faded khaki pants and sturdy hiking boots completed the look, and Kira found herself wanting to go to him and crawl onto his lap to snuggle in for a moment. When he reached into his pocket and pulled out a pair of wire-framed glasses to put on while he studied the document in front of him, Kira's mouth went dry. A pair of glasses should not seem so sexy, and yet…

"There's a fine lass to brighten up a cloudy day!" Mr. Murphy beckoned to her from his perch on the stool at the end of the bar. Grateful for a moment to collect herself lest she collapse in a puddle of lust in front of Brogan's table, Kira sauntered over to Mr. Murphy and bent to place a smacking kiss on his cheek.

"You are looking as dapper as ever, Mr. Murphy."

"Go on now. It must be my new hat. One of them fancy fae gave it to me for Christmas."

"Did he now? Then you're certainly blessed." Kira laughed with him, but she was already framing up her shot in her mind, studying the light from the window behind him. Her fingers itched for her camera, but for once, she'd left it at home.

"That's my thought, as well. Did I tell you that Cait took me to see the elephants?"

"So I heard. I've seen them as well. I did a photo study on them for *National Geographic*. Stunning animals, aren't they?"

"It was an honor to be in their presence. Majestic beasts. Truly."

"Aye, it was a beauty of a trip, wasn't it then, Mr. Murphy?" Cait came to their corner of the bar and smiled at the both of them. She could've still been twenty years of age, Kira mused, for all the lines she had in her face. Energy seemed to crackle around Cait, and Kira had always wondered if the woman ever sat still.

"It was. You'll have to show Kira your pictures."

"I'd love to see them. Speaking of pictures... Mr. Murphy, would you mind if I took your portrait?"

"My portrait? My, that sounds fancy, doesn't it, Cait?"

"It certainly does, Mr. Murphy. Have you had a proper portrait done?"

"What in the world would I do with that?" A pink tinge colored Mr. Murphy's cheeks.

"Sure and I'd put it right over the bar, I would." Cait gestured to the wall behind her. Looking up at Kira, she nodded. "You take a nice picture of him and I'll buy it from you."

"That's ridiculous. I'd gift it to you."

"I insist."

"I'll take a trade then. A few lovely meals for a photo."

"I suspect you command a fair price for your photos. More than a few meals."

"Friendly discount then." Kira stared Cait down until Cait laughed and shrugged.

"Your man's staring at you."

"Is he?" It took every ounce of willpower not to turn around and look at Brogan.

"Is he your man?" Mr. Murphy's eyes twinkled as he took another sip from his Guinness. "I was wondering which lass would land him. There's been quite a stir among the village about him."

"Has there now? I haven't heard any of the talk."

"You know how it is. Fresh blood in town," Cait said, wiping down the bar top in front of them with a rag. "There's talk about you too."

"Me? I'm from here," Kira said.

"You're beautiful and unattached," Mr. Murphy said. "The lads are also talking."

"I had no idea I was the topic of conversation." Kira tried to decide if it bothered her or not. When she'd first returned, perhaps it would have. But after weeks of being back home? Now she'd fallen into the rhythm and chatter of daily life in a small town.

"A pretty lass such as yourself? If I was thirty years younger..." Mr. Murphy mused.

"More like fifty years younger," Cait quipped.

"What's a few decades here and there?"

"I'll take a cider when you have a chance, Cait."

"I'll bring it over. Any food?"

"I'd love some of your veggie pot pie." Kira had spotted the special on the menu when she'd walked in.

"I'll bring it to you. Go on then, don't leave your man there too long or the vultures will swoop in." Cait nodded to where a giggling table of ladies studied Brogan openly.

Kira wondered if he'd even noticed that he was the focus of attention. Doubtful, she thought as she crossed the floor and stood by his table. It took a full thirty seconds before he started and looked up. Instantly, a wash of pleasure filled his face at seeing her and Kira's stomach did that funny little dance again.

"Kira, you look lovely today."

"Well, thank you. You're looking well yourself."

"Thank you. Can I get you something from the bar?"

"Cait's got me sorted, thanks."

"Please, sit. I think I've gotten myself a bit twisted about here." Brogan leaned back and took his glasses off, much to Kira's disappointment, and put them on the table by the stack of papers he'd been devouring.

"How so?"

"I've gotten quite stuck on names, logos, designs…it's just not in my wheelhouse. But I feel like I need something to name the project so I can move forward. Is that weird? It's just a sticking point for me. I need to cross it off the list so I can let the rest flow."

"Why don't you show me what you have so far?"

"I'd like to hear as well," Dylan said from where he'd come to stand by the table.

Kira sighed. So much for a moment of alone time with Brogan. She rolled her eyes as she saw Gracie, Liam, and Fi following along.

"Go on then, move over," Gracie said, unceremoniously plopping down next to Kira and bumping her over. Annoyed, Kira scooted across the U-shaped booth until she was all but pressed to Brogan's side as the others piled in. Her annoyance quickly vanished as her other senses picked up and that strange current of energy hummed between her and Brogan. She wondered if he could feel it when they were close as well.

"Oh, hello everyone. I didn't know you'd all be joining us." Brogan looked a little unnerved at the intrusion.

"As you'll quickly learn here, mate, the ladies do not like to be left out of anything," Dylan supplied. "This lovely lass is my wife, Gracie. And this other lovely lass is Liam's fiancée, Fi."

"Nice to meet you both." Brogan smiled at the women. Kira could tell when both of the women decided they liked him, as the tension in their shoulders eased at the same time.

"You don't mind us joining you then?" Fi queried.

"All hands on deck," Brogan joked. "I was just telling Kira I've worked myself into a bit of a knot. I know my strengths, and I know my weaknesses. And I'd say that designing a logo and creating a catchy name is a weakness. I'm used to being overly specific in my studies, but I can't exactly call the center 'A Location Where the Education and Enjoyment of Nature Is Promoted.'"

"That does sound a bit stiff," Kira admitted.

Brogan laughed. "Don't I know it."

"Why don't we talk about your vision first?" Dylan asked. "We're a mixed bag when it comes to our talents, and I'm sure between the lot of us we'll have you sorted out shortly."

"Well, I'm a bit torn on the totality of the vision, but I'll start with some ideas I've been kicking about. First is whether to turn Gran's cottage into the nature center itself, or live in the cottage and build a space nearby. Because it's a ways out from the village, I was thinking of the logistics of it all. I don't think people will just pass through as opposed to making a day of it, so we'll likely want to have some of the necessary creature comforts like public toilets, picnic tables – maybe a small café? Pies and a pot of tea? Then there's the trails to build, the levels of hiking abilities and so on. Oh, and the displays! Birding, flowers, ocean shells…" Brogan trailed off and blinked up at everyone, while they looked at him in silence. "What? Bad ideas?"

"No, marvelous ideas, actually." Gracie beamed at him. "And to imagine a café nearby where I don't always have to cook? Rosie and I could have a walk there and get a bite to eat when we need a breath of fresh air."

"And Flynn would likely be able to offer you fresh catch," Dylan supplied, speaking of Gracie's father.

"Of course he would. And what about relics in the area? Like any old stone tools people find or arrowheads, that kind of thing?"

"Um…" Brogan said, but Gracie barreled right over him.

"You could also have a literature section discussing the myths and legends of the area. Maybe a spot for people who aren't going on a hike to sit and read while they wait for the rest of the group? Or a lending library?"

"Sure, that's –" Brogan said.

"You'll need a gift shop, as well. You could sell prints and some of Gracie's all-natural tonics and creams."

"Right." Brogan sat back and exhaled.

"Have a drink, mate." Liam gestured to Brogan's pint.

"Ladies, these are all great ideas. But first, let's focus on a few things we need to discuss, and then we can help Brogan with a name and a logo. Why don't you two spend some time thinking on that while we discuss a few matters?" A natural manager, Dylan delegated tasks quickly.

Fi and Gracie pulled out a sheet of paper and bent their heads together over it, while Kira sat back and took a sip of cider from the glass Cait had placed in front of her. She could just picture the nature center in her mind, a happy little hub of education and exploration, another tourist draw for this part of Ireland. It would be good. Really good, Kira thought, and pulled her mind back to the conversation at hand.

"Brogan, I've been able to track down who's behind the housing development. It turns out it's a Dublin-owned company named McCarthy Investments. They've taken to doing these types of developments all over Ireland – building up new housing with cheap materials, charging too much for the places, and not paying much attention to any sort of zoning laws. They've already several lawsuits against them, so we'd be adding to it. However, because we've an in with the local law enforcement, we could actually physically stop the construction here. I've taken the liberty of speaking with the Gardaí in regard to that and they said they would be willing to stop construction so long as we can supply the appropriate papers."

"Aye, I've just received the surveyor's report today. They're on a large corner of my land." Brogan pulled a cardboard tube from his side, and slid rolled papers from it. Together the men bent over the drawings to look.

"Sure and they're cheeky, aren't they? They're clear onto your land." Liam stroked his beard as he studied the lines of the map. "That's going to cost them."

"The good thing is that from what I can see they've only dug up the land; they haven't actually started building yet. It looks like that's the next phase."

Liam and Dylan glanced at each other.

"Are you thinking what I'm thinking, mate?" Liam asked.

"Aye. Emergency fencing. We'll have David on it by morning."

"Emergency fencing?"

"It's basically a temporary permit restriction with police backing on it. When we put it up, if construction continues, we can triple our fines which will cost the firm a pretty penny in fees." Dylan smiled.

"Plus, I had a chat with the lads working on the Community Center in town," Liam said. "Seems that they do know a few of the men working on the project. Apparently, the employer isn't on site and doesn't pay a fair wage. Which means…"

"The workers won't risk getting in trouble with the police to push through on the construction," Brogan said.

"Right, boyo. I think we'll get this locked up in short order. But Gracie said something about otters?"

Gracie looked up at her name and then nodded at Kira.

"We need to see how the construction has diverted the water source to the pond that's closer to your place," Kira said.

"I had a look at it, actually." Brogan pointed to a spot on the map. "It's just here. One of the few spots they *have* built on my land. They put up drainage pipes and a wall. It looks like they were going to redirect or filter the water for some purpose. Either way, if we can break it down and smooth it out, we should be able to redirect the natural flow of the river down the hills once more. It looks like it's gone almost completely dry in the riverbed. A few dry weeks and Fergal's pond will dry up as well."

"Fergal?" Liam asked.

"I named him," Kira laughed.

"Well, 'tis a fine name for an otter." Accustomed by now to the whims of the women of Grace's Cove, Liam just smiled at Kira.

"He says he needs our help, so we'll do what we can," Brogan muttered, still looking down at the map. All eyes at the table turned to Brogan and then landed on Kira.

"Did he say that then?" Liam asked lightly.

"Oh, well, um…" Brogan looked up, a faint blush heating his cheeks as he realized all eyes were back on him. Caught, and clearly not wanting to out Kira, he shrugged. "I could just tell he needed help."

It warmed Kira that he would automatically protect her, not knowing what she had shared of herself with others, and it made her realize just how good his character was.

"I've told him about my abilities, guys. It's okay." Kira reached out and squeezed Brogan's arm. "Thank you for protecting me, but my family knows about me."

"You've told him?" Fi looked surprised. "Well, I suppose he'll have to get used to us, anyway, won't he? Particularly when Gracie flies into a snit. The whole town knows when she's in a mood."

"I resent that," Gracie said, her eyes flashing. A clap of thunder sounded over the pub and Cait shot a warning look at their table.

"There better be no fighting in this pub, you hear me, Gracie?" Cait called.

"I'm not on to have a fight," Gracie mumbled, burying her face in her whiskey.

"Wait…" Brogan sat back and looked between the ladies.

"But I haven't yet told him about the rest of us." Kira widened her eyes and gave a meaningful look across the table to Gracie. "Let's try not to scare him away now, shall we?"

"If you talking to animals and reading objects doesn't scare him off, I don't suppose a bit of other magick would either – right, Brogan?" Gracie sent Brogan a silky smile. "Surely you're made of stronger stuff than that."

Brogan looked flummoxed. "I…"

"Give him a moment to digest." Dylan smiled at his wife. "Not everyone processes at the rate you do."

"Well, surely his gran told him of the cove. She was close friends with Fiona, wasn't she? There's no way he hasn't heard some talk of magick and whatnot through the years."

"Aye, she did tell me. Plus, Fiona paid me a visit the other day. So I'm supposing it's only natural there's more magick afoot in Grace's Cove. It wouldn't make sense that you're the only one, right?" Brogan smiled down at Kira and she felt the breath leave her in a little whoosh of air. Who was this gentle and accommodating man? No judgment, just easy acceptance of what was. For a scientist, she was surprised he wasn't offering more pushback.

Gracie seemed to read Kira's thoughts. "You're a scientist, aren't you? Typically your kind is a difficult lot to convince."

"I can well see that. I am a scientist – but I'm also Catherine's grandson, and I'm Irish. It wouldn't do to not have at least a bit of a belief in mysticism, right?"

"I like him," Fi said, speaking directly to Kira as if Brogan wasn't there.

"Me too. You should keep him, Kira," Gracie urged.

"Ladies, that's enough matchmaking. We have other issues to discuss. Like how we're going to get this fence up, save the otters, and start building a nature center. I believe I gave you a task to do?" Dylan interjected, neatly rescuing Fi and Gracie before Kira jumped across the table and murdered the both of them.

"Right. We've come up with a few ideas, but these are the favorites so far." Fi nodded at Gracie.

"Mystic Nature Center, Catherine's Conservatory, or O'Hallahan's Oasis."

Brogan beamed at them. "For my gran!"

"I like O'Hallahan's Oasis. It sounds welcoming, like a

spot you'd want to spend time in, not just a boring infor-
mational center with no life to it," Kira said.

"I like it as well," Brogan said.

"I say move forward with that name and if a better one
pops up, so be it," Dylan proposed. "That way, you'll have
a working name and it won't be a roadblock in your head
anymore."

"That works for me."

Gracie had opened her mouth, likely to badger Brogan
with more questions, but Dylan neatly overrode her by
asking, "Do you have a budget for the project?"

"That's an area I could use some help with. I've
outlined what I think will be the basic necessities, along
with a general design for the center. But I'll need architects
and so on to weigh in on costs."

"Why don't I take what you have and get back to
you?" Liam asked. "I've a good eye for all these things
and can likely get you a better idea of costs, timelines, and
project necessities within the week."

"That would be great. You all are being so nice to me.
You don't have to take any of this on, you know," Brogan
protested. "I can hire help in."

"Nonsense. You're one of us, Brogan, even if you
weren't raised here. Fiona would be slapping us upside
the head if we didn't offer to help her friend's grandson
with such a noble project. Speaking of which," Gracie
said, ignoring Dylan's warning look, "you said Fiona
paid you a visit? Are we speaking of the same Fiona,
then?"

"Young, buxom, easy with her wiles?" Brogan asked,
cupping his hands in front of his chest.

"I withdraw my earlier statement about liking you," Gracie said, ice coating her tone.

Brogan threw back his head and laughed, the sound sending little trills of pleasure through Kira's body.

"If by Fiona you mean the spirit who visited me and gave me a talking to, then yes."

"That would be the one. She didn't send you running for the hills, then?"

"Aye, she spooked me. But it was nice to hear that Gran's faring well."

"You believed in her then?" Kira looked at him in question. "Just like that?"

"It's hard to ignore what's right in front of my eyes, isn't it?" Heat flashed behind Brogan's eyes as he studied her, and Kira's mouth went dry at his words. Did he mean more than what he was saying? She certainly hoped so.

"Well then," Gracie amended, "I stick by my earlier statement – I like you."

"I like you, too," Brogan said.

But his eyes never left Kira's.

CHAPTER 17

*K*ira couldn't remember when she'd ever been so busy before. Usually, when she was on shoots, there was typically a lot of downtime and prep work followed by a few long days of shooting. But between helping to run the gallery and the nature center, Kira found her days zipping by in a flurry of emails and text messages.

However, everything was coming together.

More than anything, Kira was surprised by how much she was enjoying being involved in the nuts and bolts of building something. While her brain ran toward the creative side of things, she'd found that also meant she had a skill for creative problem solving. More than once, she'd gone head-to-head with Brogan over some seemingly inconsequential detail. She often got her way, but not always. However, it was more than their shared goal that was keeping her mind occupied these days.

Kira was falling for Brogan – big time.

While he could be maddeningly thorough at times,

when she wanted to race ahead to an end point, Brogan was slowly teaching her the patience that was needed when it came to building something step-by-step. Even when they argued, he'd logically and calmly build his case, to the point where Kira began escalating her arguments just to see if she could get him to lose his cool. The heat she'd seen flash behind his eyes when he looked at her was still there, yet not once had he lost control of his emotions with her.

Nor had he kissed her again.

That point was driving her particularly crazy. It was like she'd been given a sample taste of a new item at the market, and then it sold out before she could buy more. The more she was around Brogan, the more Kira wanted her hands on him. Or her mouth. She'd taken to accidently brushing against him here and there, just to feel the tingle of electricity that coursed between them. He'd become like a drug, and Kira craved more interaction.

And yet, Brogan plodded on, focused on his nature center, calmly working on the plans as though he hadn't a care in the world. She was beginning to wonder if he even really saw her anymore, or if she'd been relegated to just a friend and business partner.

It was enough to drive a woman mad, Kira thought as she drove toward the trail to the pond. Brogan had texted her and asked her to meet him there at her convenience. Like a bloody business associate. Was he really going to act like they'd never shared a moment or two together? That their kisses never happened?

"Maybe it's because he's one of those people who don't like to mix work and pleasure. Now that he's all in with the nature center and you're working with him – perhaps he doesn't want to muddy the waters? I can understand that. It's a difficult line to walk," Fi had said.

"Wouldn't you think he'd address it then? Put it out on the table? Say something – anything at all?" Kira had groused.

"Well, you haven't addressed it either, have you?"

"But… why… I mean, no, I haven't."

"He strikes me as a bit shy, Kira. And you're… well, you're a force to be reckoned with."

"Are you saying I scare him?" Kira glared at Fi.

"You're scaring me right now and I know you well. So, aye, I'm saying stop being scary. If you want to know what's going on in his head – just ask him."

Kira sniffed at the thought as she pulled her car to a stop. Like she could ask Brogan why he'd kissed her so that all her senses had screamed in high alert, but now treated her like a kid sister. The man would push his glasses up his nose and peer at her in confusion.

Goddess above, but she loved when he pulled his glasses from his pocket and perched them on his nose. Never in a million years would she have thought she'd have the hots for a nerdy scientist who calmly managed spreadsheets like they weren't tools of the devil himself. And yet, here she was.

More than a little cranky, Kira huffed her way up the path, narrowing her eyes at the dark clouds that hovered on the horizon.

"You just go on and stay over there," Kira muttered to the clouds. Rounding a curve in the trail, she found Brogan leaning on a low stone wall. Her heart did a little dance at the sight of him, his broad shoulders tucked into his trim red jacket, a few errant curls poking out from beneath his knit cap. He needed a haircut, Kira thought – and a smack upside the head.

"You do know I have work to be doing, right?"

"And hello to you as well, lovely Miss Kira. A delight it is to see you on this grey day." Brogan's grin flashed white in his face.

"Right. What are you needing then?" Kira refused to be charmed.

"Is something wrong?" Seeing that he couldn't tease her from her mood, a worried look crossed Brogan's face. "Are there problems at the gallery? Am I asking too much of your time?"

"No." Kira sighed and squeezed the bridge of her nose. "I'm just in a mood. What is it I can help you with today, Brogan?"

"I'm sorry. Is there anything I can do to help you feel better?" Brogan, methodically as ever, didn't move from his spot on the wall.

Kiss me, Kira thought. But she waved away his question with a small sigh. "It's a funk I'm in. It happens sometimes. I'll be just fine. It's the artistic temperament and all."

"Ah, right. Is this where you throw things and insist that nobody understands your vision?" Brogan teased lightly.

"Something like that." Despite herself, Kira felt a smile tugging at her lips. She'd never been one for temper tantrums – she'd leave that particular award to Gracie. But she could see the merit in how satisfying they must feel.

Not all the time, but maybe just once in a while to let off steam.

"Here." Brogan bent over, then handed her a rock.

"What's this for?"

"To throw."

"Oh, you think you're funny?" Kira held it up and mocked like she was going to throw it at his head. Brogan smiled and held up his hands playfully.

"Give it a go. Preferably not at my head."

"All right then." Kira launched the stone across the field, where it hit a pile of rocks and tumbled satisfactorily down the side of a hill.

"And?"

"I suppose that feels good."

"We can stay here as long as you need and throw as many stones as you want." Brogan regarded her patiently.

"I think I'm good. I promise."

"You sure? I don't want you scaring poor Fergal. He's my buddy now, too."

"Do you visit him often?" Kira asked, falling into step beside Brogan as they hiked up the hill toward the pond.

"Almost every day."

"You do?" Kira stopped and looked up at Brogan. "Really? I'm surprised."

"He's cool. I like watching him move in the water and all his cute little mannerisms. I feel like he's come to trust me, so he doesn't hide when I'm around anymore."

"You're bringing him fish, aren't you?"

"Not all the time. I've told him he can't rely on me as a food source since I won't always be able to visit. I'm not sure he understands, but…"

"He understands." Kira thought about Brogan up here, talking to an otter, keeping him company and making sure he was safe. If her heart wasn't already lost to him, now it slid over the final drop-off.

"Really? Even if I don't have your powers?" Brogan asked, his tone holding no hint of censure, only curiosity.

"That doesn't bother you, does it?" Kira stopped on the trail once again, and Brogan walked a few more steps before realizing she wasn't following. Turning, he looked down at her and Kira's stomach flipped. The way his eyes studied hers in a careful manner, as though he was pulling her apart layer by layer, made a trickle of sweat break out across her brow. It was like he was seeing her, *really* seeing her, in a way that she hadn't allowed anyone to before. She was so used to having a camera in hand that it had become her wall, her protection; it kept people back because she was always the one in control of what she wanted people to see.

But this man with kind blue eyes, desperately in need of a haircut and a shave, patiently saw his way through her defenses.

"That I can't speak to Fergal?" Brogan winked at her so she knew he was joking.

"You know what I mean." Kira smiled. "The magick. You seemed to take it in stride that there were more of us with power at the table at Gallagher's."

"I figured if Dylan and Liam haven't run for their lives already, I'm likely just fine."

"What if they've been charmed? Put under a spell?" Kira tested him.

"First, do no harm, right?"

"Oh, wow, someone's been doing a little research then, hasn't he?" Kira couldn't decide if she was impressed or annoyed that he hadn't come to her with his questions.

"I thought it would behoove me to read up on the subject as it seems I'll be surrounded by those who were gifted with a little something extra."

"And that's it, then? It doesn't bother you? You don't think we're weird? It's 'gifts' to you and not a curse from the devil or something like that?" Kira had heard it all in her time.

"First of all, I'm not one to believe in the devil, though I'll have to rethink that now that I know there's a world of magick out there," Brogan mused, looking faintly piqued that it hadn't occurred to him to research this sooner. "Secondly, I'm not one to be judging anyone else's weirdness as I've always been a bit of an oddball myself. If you're looking for judgement or condemnation, it won't be coming from me."

"But – okay, well, take emotions and past history out of it. What about your science mind? Doesn't it seek to prove us wrong?" A blast of wind buffeted down the hills, shaking Kira and pushing her a step closer to Brogan.

"A scientific mind is one that seeks to understand. Frankly, we're kind of renegades when you think about it. Science doesn't just try to follow the rules – it seeks to break the rules. To define new rules. New parameters. To form new understandings. It wouldn't be very science-minded of me if I just dismissed something that I can't immediately understand. Instead, I'm looking to expand my knowledge on it."

"But... without judgement? You're fine with me

talking to animals and picking up things and reading their history?"

"Of course; why wouldn't I be? Have I given you any indication that I disrespect you or your powers? If so, my deepest apologies. I certainly didn't mean to be conveying that impression if that's the one you've received." Concern flashed across Brogan's face, and he stepped forward to lean closer to Kira. "I think you're wonderful, Kira. Full stop. No condemnation. No judgement. But… perhaps a lot of questions. I'm a curious sort by nature, I suppose."

"You can ask all the questions you'd like." Kira huffed out a laugh, feeling a little knot inside of her loosen. She wasn't sure how much more she could hammer him with this question – he'd answered honestly and his aura reflected that.

Stop looking for problems or criticisms that aren't there, Kira scolded herself.

"Oh, I plan to." Brogan waited a moment longer to see if Kira had anything else to say. It was something else she had noticed about him. He was patient with his listening and always waited to see if someone had finished making their point.

"Carry on, good sir," Kira said.

"Perfect. I hope you'll enjoy what I have to show you today."

"Have you trained Fergal to jump through hoops?"

"Alas, not yet. We're working on it, though. He's our opening act for the ribbon-cutting ceremony when we open the nature center."

Kira laughed. "He's going to be famous."

"He already is, thanks to your Instagram. I can't believe how many people are attached to otters."

"I can't either. I mean, I can, but still…" Kira shook her head. In Otter News' Instagram page had grown to thirty thousand followers over the past few weeks. She thought about how long it had taken to build up her own professional social media following, and how quickly a cute otter had just dominated Instagram. It was enough to humble a person, it was.

"It's not just Fergal, though he is cute. It's your photos. You really capture the essence of him. You've made otters seem almost like our friends."

"They are – if we treat them with respect and don't demand anything from them."

"I suppose that's a good rule for any friendship, isn't it?" Brogan smiled over his shoulder at her as they reached the cusp of the hill just before the pond. "Okay, close your eyes. I'll guide you."

"Oh, a proper surprise? Grand." Kira smiled and let Brogan take her hands.

She didn't put her shields up fast enough and the essence of Brogan washed through Kira. His emotions pummeled her – excitement, nerves, shyness… and was that a healthy dose of lust? Kira slammed the wall down before she read too much from Brogan. It was a point of pride of hers to never read someone unintentionally. Other-wise, nobody in her life would ever be able to have any privacy.

"Ready? You can open your eyes." Brogan dropped her hands, as Kira still whirled from the rush of his emotions.

For a moment, she kept her eyes closed to steady herself and clear her head. A sound greeted her... like...

"Is that running water?" Kira's eyes popped open in excitement and she clapped her hands in front of herself at the sight that greeted her.

A river, an actual flowing river – well, a waterfall really – poured over the side of the ledge and into Fergal's pond. The pond itself had almost doubled in size, and Kira could see now just how low the water level had become for Fergal. On the other side of the pond, two new additions had been added.

"I can't believe it! The water is back!" Kira squealed. "And did you add a bench and – what *is* that?"

"Come see." Brogan grabbed her hand again and all but dragged her around the pond. Kira was too focused on the miraculous change to the area to read Brogan's emotions.

"Seriously, what *is* this?" Kira laughed at a little stone structure half-submerged in the water. The dome-shaped stone had arches on all sides for the water to flow through. There was writing inscribed on the top, and Kira leaned over to read it. "Fergal's Fortress? Oh my goddess, did you make Fergal a fort?"

"I did!" Brogan rocked back on his heels, pleased with himself. "I thought he might like a little spot to hang out in that could protect him from the elements if need be."

"I love it!" Kira's heart tripped when Fergal's little face poked out of an archway in his fortress. "Fergal!"

Friends. Man is nice.

"Fergal, are you happy? We brought the water back to you. Is this better?"

Kira crouched at the side of the water.

Much better. Mate.

"Mate?" Kira asked, and tears sprang unbidden to her eyes when another furry head popped up next to Fergal's. "Oh, Fergal. Is this your mate? She's lovely. Nice to meet you."

Friend? Fergal's mate asked.

"Friend. I can understand you. I'm so happy you and Fergal are together. Do you have a name?"

The otter looked around and then focused on a flower budding by the pond.

Heather.

"That's lovely then. I'm so happy for you both. I hope you'll enjoy the pond together."

Thank you.

"He did it." Kira pointed to Brogan. "Remember, he is a friend. He saved your home. He may bring people by for a while to learn about you both, but never to harm. Understood?"

We like people. If they are nice. Or have fish.

"They say they like people if they are nice or bring fish." Kira turned to find Brogan sitting on the bench, an unnameable emotion in his eyes as he watched her. Crossing to him, she sat down close enough that their shoulders touched. For a moment, they sat in silence, watching as the otters dived in the pond, clearly delighted with their new digs.

"I'm glad they're happy. It wasn't easy to deal with, but Dylan and Liam are a force of nature. They pretty much steamrolled the developer and had the river moved in a matter of days. I've never seen anything like it."

"It's a particular trait they both have. Dylan will plow through people. Liam will charm them until they don't know what happened. Either way, they're known for getting things done."

"I'm grateful to them. They don't even know me. You didn't really, either. And yet, you've all welcomed me in so easily. It's…"

Kira heard a catch in his voice, and found her tears hovering at her eyes again. He didn't need to say what she already knew he felt deep inside. For the first time, Brogan felt like he had a family. Wanting him more than she could control, Kira turned and laid a hand against his cheek, nudging his face until he looked at her. She'd been right about the catch in his voice – a faint sheen highlighted his eyes.

Leaning forward, she did the only thing she could do in this moment: She kissed him.

At first, the moment held suspended, their lips pressed softly together, that lovely hum of energy flowing between them. But when Brogan went to pull back, Kira pushed forward, wrapping her arms around his neck and leaning in to deepen the kiss. Brogan paused for a moment, and she coaxed him with her lips, inviting him to lose a tiny fraction of his control, to reveal himself to her.

She knew the instant Brogan relented. His hands came up and threaded through her hair. Tilting her head, he pulled her closer, opening her lips with his tongue to explore gently. Heat flashed between them, and a knowing.

This one, Kira thought. This was the man she'd spent her whole life searching for. He swept her under with his kisses, his gentle exploration only feeding the fire that burned deep inside her, making her desperate. When he pulled away, Kira whimpered against him, her heart racing, her body demanding more. Leaning into him, Kira buried her face into the crook of his neck for a moment, enjoying the feel of his arms cradling her close. She wanted all of him, Kira realized. Not just stolen kisses that left her aching instead of satiating her hunger.

"Brogan… I…"

The dark clouds she'd warned away before broke open above them, and once more, Kira found herself and Brogan running from the deluge of rain that all but blinded them. Annoyed, Kira shook her fist at the sky as she sprinted for her car.

It was Mother Nature's version of taking a cold shower.

CHAPTER 18

"*A*ren't you in a fine huff today?"

Brogan dropped the mug he was holding and it shattered at his feet. Wincing, Brogan stepped back and looked down at his bare feet and the shards of porcelain on the floor in front of him.

"Sure and it's a fine time to surprise a body, isn't it then?" Brogan glared at Fiona, who had materialized in the kitchen of his gran's cottage. He wore nothing but a towel wrapped loosely around his waist, and he'd just poured himself a second cup of coffee to take the edges off the mood left by a fitful night of sleep.

"Did you cut yourself?" Fiona ignored the question of her inopportune timing.

"I don't think so. And luckily, I'd left the pot of coffee off, or I'd be scalded." Annoyed, Brogan shot Fiona a glare and stepped carefully backward until he could reach the broom and dustpan hanging by the counter. Fiona said nothing as he tidied the floor. Standing, he dumped the contents in the bin and then shot Fiona another mutinous look. "You stay right there. I'm putting clothes on and then I'll have a word with you."

"Yes, sir." Fiona's eyes lit with laughter but she knew better than to poke the bear.

Of all the things, Brogan groused to himself as he stuck his legs back in the shower and rinsed the coffee from them. He'd tortured himself all night with wicked thoughts of Kira in his arms, and how he wanted to discover her body inch by inch. Their kiss yesterday had blown his mind, leaving him reeling and more than a little worked up. If the skies hadn't opened up on them again, he might have ignored Fiona's warning about taking it slow and tried to have his way with Kira right then and there.

Though, he supposed the rain had been a saving grace, Brogan thought as he dug into his wardrobe and pulled out pants, a sweatshirt in soft grey, and thick wool cottage socks. He couldn't imagine what Fergal would have thought if he'd pushed the limits with Kira in front of him.

And here he was considering the feelings of an otter. Brogan squeezed the bridge of his nose and took a few deep, calming breaths. Ever since the day he'd stepped into the gallery and been bowled over by Kira, his nerves had been like a plucked guitar string. It wasn't a feeling he was comfortable with, and he was worried he was being positively maudlin these days. What with almost crying in front of Kira over how kind people had been to him here, to trying not to rush Kira into a relationship, Brogan wasn't sure he was in control of *any* of his emotions anymore.

"Well? What has brought you here at this fine hour? Surely it wasn't just to see me in my towel," Brogan grumbled at Fiona when he returned to the kitchen. Luckily there was still enough coffee in the pot for one more luke-warm cup, and Brogan poured himself a new mug. Turn-ing, he leaned against the counter and studied the ghost who hovered, a guilty look on her face, by the small kitchen table covered in his gran's lace doilies.

"While that happened to be fine luck on my part, no, it wasn't just to ogle your muscles." Fiona grinned at him, clearly pleased by his attitude. "I sensed your angst – it's getting worse, you know – so I wanted to be checking in with you to ask how you are. Your gran sends her love, by the way."

"Does she now? You could be just saying that to make me be nicer to you." Still annoyed, Brogan sipped his coffee.

"I could be. Hm. Let's see what else she's said, so you know it's her. Oh – she thinks O'Hallahan's Oasis is the best name, and she appreciates you honoring her in that way. She'd like it if you would maybe think about living in her cottage instead of turning it into the nature center. She thinks you'd be happy here. And she suggested that the area by her garden shed – behind it, you know? The land is flat there and gets good light. It would be great for a photography studio."

"A photography… she thinks for Kira? To work out here?"

"For you both to live here. Together. She likes Kira. A lot. I can't be blaming her, either. Kira's of my blood, and I love her dearly."

"Oh sure, well, you've both got it all figured out now, don't you? What about what I want? Hmm? Any of that fall under consideration? Or I should just go in line with what a ghost who pops into my kitchen tells me. Because I'll be honest, it's not working out so well for me, now is it?"

"Well, my dear, what do you want, then?" Fiona's lips quirked.

"You well know what I want. And I took your advice to go slow. But now I want Kira more than ever and the slower I go with her, the more I realize she's... well, she's beyond me."

"Why do you say that?"

"Kira is like... she's like a flame. It needs constant tending to keep the fire going. I'm worried I won't have enough kindling to keep her fire hot." Brogan took another gulp of coffee before continuing. "I'm not sure if that makes sense. But she's... she's *alive*, in a busy and frenetic way. I'm pragmatic, thorough, and definitely not a high-energy rock star. I worry she'll tire of me."

"Ah. So you're keeping her at bay because you're worried she'll reject you?"

"Well, initially, I was going slow based on your recommendation. Now, I like her so much that I'm worried I'll lose her forever if we date. I'd rather have her in my life in any capacity than not at all, so I'm thinking that I may just have to keep her as a friend and business partner only."

"You sell yourself short." Fiona floated closer to him, genuine concern on her face. "You'd be a brilliant partner for Kira. As a friend, a mate, and a lover. You can fight this because of your own insecurities if you like, but I'll tell you – fate has a way of picking up the reins."

"You're saying we're fated?"

158 TRICIA O'MALLEY

"I'm saying be careful not to refuse a gift, lest it's something you've needed all along."

"But…" Brogan blinked at the empty space in front of him. "Oh, lovely. Another woman who needs the last word."

His phone buzzed on the table and he picked it up.

A text from Liam: *Beers tonight?* Brogan thought about it and realized that a night with the lads might be just what he needed.

Sure, where? Out here?

Come to town. You can crash on Dylan's boat if you're not one to be seasick.

Ah. A proper night of beers. Yes, much needed. See you later.

There. A lads' night was exactly what Brogan needed to keep his mind off of one leather-and-lace-wearing enchanting woman who had put a spell on him, whether she'd meant to or not.

"WOMEN ARE THE WORST." Brogan squinted one eye as he tried to focus on the dartboard. They were in Liam and Fi's downstairs apartment, located on the waterfront of Grace's Cove. The two lived upstairs and had converted the downstairs into an office space for Fi and a hang-out area for Liam, who liked to come here for a drink, he said, when he didn't want the whole town listening in on his business. A wise man, that Liam.

"Sure and it's fine if you're into men, then. But Dylan

and I are both taken." Liam whistled as Brogan hit the bullseye.

"I sometimes wonder if it would be easier. No games. Straightforward communication. No fuss."

"Mmm, I don't know. I think that, like with anything, it depends on the person. I've known many a man who was a bloody nightmare to get a straight answer from," Dylan said. He took the darts from Brogan and stood at the line to throw. "Grass is always greener, and all that."

"Here's another one for you." Liam poured a generous helping of whiskey into Brogan's glass. "Might as well keep drinking if you're considering changing teams."

"I'm not. I'm just…"

"Frustrated? Mooning after our pretty Kira?"

"I am *not* mooning," Brogan scoffed.

"What seems to be the issue then? She appears to like you, from what I can tell." Liam plopped down on his leather couch and propped a foot on his knee. "Sláinte."

Brogan held his glass in the air before taking a sip. The night had taken on a fuzzy quality, as if all the edges had rounded out, and he was feeling relaxed even though the topic of conversation was not what he'd wanted to discuss. He'd thought he'd get out, have some pints, and ignore anything to do with womenfolk.

"She's just a friend."

"Is she now?" Dylan laughed and shook his head, neatly throwing his darts. "That's game, by the way."

"Bollocks," Brogan muttered. Plopping into a low-slung chair by the window, he took another sip of his whiskey. The liquid burned down to his core, warming him and helping to make sense of the muddle of thoughts in his brain.

"You're saying you've no interest in Kira? I read that situation wrong," Liam said, reaching up to scratch his beard.

"Oh. I'm interested. I just can't *be* interested. We're working together now. Best not to go there."

"I heard from a little bird that you've already gone there," Dylan said, cheerfully throwing Gracie under the bus.

"We've kissed, yes. But it has to stop there. Initially, I thought there could be more, but now... I don't know. Fiona told me to take it slow. So I did. And now I'm terrified that..." Brogan broke off.

"Ah, we were wondering what Fiona paid you a visit for. You didn't elaborate the other night," Dylan said. He'd topped off his own glass and settled in next to Liam.

"Does she visit you too?" Brogan changed the subject before he started blubbering on the floor about Kira and got his man-card revoked.

"Fiona? From time to time. More at my home, much to both Gracie's and my annoyance. Well, I don't mind it so much, but I don't always see her. She and Gracie have a running battle over every ingredient Gracie uses in her healing creams. Frankly, I think Gracie likes having someone to argue with all day, since she's alone in the cottage doing her work."

"And that's just... that's the norm now?" Brogan held out his hand in the air and made a little circle with it. "All the magick and stuff?"

"Sure and it's unusual. But you adjust in time." Liam

smiled at Brogan. "When you love someone, you have to accept who they are without asking them to change for you. Kira can no more stop her abilities than you could force yourself not to breathe. It's just who she is."

"I'm not asking her to change. I don't want her to change. She's... perfect." Brogan sighed.

Liam and Dylan exchanged looks.

"Does the magick of the cove scare you? Or the magick in the bloodline here? Is that it?"

"I don't know anything about the magick of the cove, other than my gran warning me to be staying out of it because it's enchanted. Are you saying the two are entwined? The cove and the women's magick?"

"Aye, they are entwined. It's passed through the blood," Dylan said. "From the great Grace O'Malley herself."

"It's not a bad thing," Liam said, a look of wonder crossing his face. "All my life, I'd been certain there were mermaids or other water nymphs. Long nights at sea almost convinced me magick was real. I cannot tell you how delighted I was to discover that something I'd once thought was the stuff of make-believe existed."

"It's a gift, Brogan. Truly. To know a world with magick in it... well, it was like going from watching a black-and-white movie to HD full-spectrum color. The possibilities are endless. And isn't that a fun life to live?" Dylan asked.

"I'm coming around to it. Frankly, I find it fascinating. I already have pages of questions that I want to ask, but I'm worried I'll annoy the ladies. I'm waiting until they know me better before I start," Brogan admitted sheepishly.

"If it's not the magick bothering you, then why aren't you making a move on Kira?"

"I... well, I had a rough upbringing, all right?" Brogan skewered the men with a look that didn't invite more questions. "I haven't had the best model for relationships, let alone how a family unit should run. You've all welcomed me in, but I... well... the way you move so easily amongst each other, comfortable in yourselves, is really eye-opening to me. I admire it."

"But you fear you can't belong?" Dylan asked.

"I do worry, yes. I'm hoping to belong here. It's already starting to feel like home." That was about as close to opening his heart as Brogan was willing to go, and the other men seemed to sense it.

"We like you, Brogan. You're one of the lads now, and that's that. But I'm still not understanding the issue with Kira."

"I think he's worried he's not good enough for her," Dylan said to Liam.

"It's not even that I'm not good enough. I'm proud of the man I've become and what I'm creating with the nature center and all. I like myself. I'm happy with where I've come in life. I just fear that I might not be enough for Kira. She's... she's a live wire. And I don't know that I'm enough electricity for her."

Both men squinted at him, trying to follow along with his muddled thoughts.

"From my experience," Liam began, as he stood and

picked up the darts, "a live wire needs to be grounded. If a live wire meets another live wire... ka-boom."

"It explodes and burns out too quickly," Dylan agreed.

"You're saying I could ground her? That sounds awful. Like I'm restricting her."

"Balancing, is what we're saying. All that lovely energy can still churn and flow, but you can help channel it."

"Huh." Brogan leaned back in his chair and finished his whiskey.

"Fill him up. I suspect he's a proper brood coming on," Dylan said, and Liam cheerfully obliged.

"Okay, lads, enough crying into our whiskey. Next one to win gets a free dinner at Gallagher's from the loser."

"You're on." Brogan stood and laughed when they cheered for him. Time to think about lady problems later. For now, he wanted to revel in a rare lads' night out.

With that, he took the darts from Dylan, determined to deliver a proper trouncing.

CHAPTER 19

*W*hat was that noise? Was someone singing outside her apartment? Kira propped herself up on her elbows in bed. She'd been trying her best to read, but her mind had constantly darted away to focus on more interesting things. Like Brogan's kisses.

The singing grew louder and Kira crinkled her forehead in confusion. There was no way somebody was in her little courtyard, was there? Sliding out from under the covers, Kira wrapped a soft flannel robe around her body and crept to the door. Opening it a crack, she peeked out.

"The fairest lass in all the land…" Brogan stood at the bottom of her steps, his hands in the air, a dopey grin on his face.

"Oh my. Brogan, what exactly are you doing?"

"I'm storming the castle, my love. Permission to board?"

"Um…" Kira laughed at his mixed metaphors. "I'm not sure you can storm the castle and also ask permission at the same time."

"Right. Storming it is."

Brogan pounded up the steps and stood in front of her, swaying lightly on his feet. When he tilted a little too far backward, Kira grabbed his arm and pulled him forward, worried he would topple down the stairs and break his neck.

"Right then," she said with a grin, "you're well and truly pissed, aren't you?"

"Aye, lassie. I had a lads' night," Brogan proclaimed and swaggered inside.

"Did you now? And you're feeling mighty proud of yourself then?" Kira moved to the little kitchenette to put a kettle on to boil.

"I won at darts. Liam was not happy."

"Did you? That's a mighty feat, it is. I'm not sure anyone's managed to beat him in quite some time. He'll be smarting about that for a while now."

"He owes me dinner. We bet and *I* won."

Kira tilted her head, smiling at how pleased Brogan looked with himself. She wondered when the last time was that he'd had a proper lads' night. It seemed like something he craved, and yet perhaps had struggled to have in his life. Grateful for the wonderful men her friends had hooked, she sent a silent thank-you to the goddesses for helping Brogan to find his way here. Whether he realized it or not, Grace's Cove was now his home.

"That's a fine achievement, it is. I'm pleased you're making friends here, Brogan." She reached up to grab mugs from the shelf for tea, and when she turned back, she bumped into his chest.

"I'm pleased I'm making friends here too, Kira. Will

you be my friend?" Brogan asked, caging her in lightly against the counter.

The scent of him, soapy mixed with a woodsy earthy smell, intoxicated her. She wanted to lean forward and press her lips to the pulse she could see hammering in his throat.

"I am your friend, Brogan," Kira said, nudging him gently back when the tea kettle began to whistle. Brogan retreated and she took a shaky breath in. The man was more than three sheets to the wind, so it was best she tread carefully, no matter how much she wanted to tackle him to her bed and have her way with him right now. She wouldn't be pleased if Brogan were to take advantage of her in such a situation, so she needed to be respectful of that. Granted, she likely wouldn't show up at Brogan's door pissed and singing songs, but to each their own, she supposed.

"It's nice here. Grace's Cove. It has its way of burrowing into your heart, doesn't it?"

"It does at that." Kira turned to find Brogan sprawled on her bed. At some point, he'd divested himself of his shoes and now rested comfortably against the headboard with a pillow propped behind him. Was this the same man who had professed shyness as a weakness? "Make yourself comfortable then."

"I am. Come join me." Brogan patted the bed.

"I don't think I need an invitation to me own bed," Kira pointed out and handed him his cup of tea. Rounding the end of the bed, she put her tea on the side table and stopped to look at him. He was almost too big for her bed, his feet reaching to the end, and he'd crossed his muscular arms behind his head. The juxtaposition of raw manliness against the feminine pink of her sheets made her itch for her camera. It wouldn't hurt, would it? Her heart pounded in her chest, being this near to him, and she wanted nothing more than to cozy up to him. Not just tonight... but every night.

"I suppose that's true. Why are you looking at me like that?"

"How do I look?"

"Like you're examining me."

"Can I take your picture? Just as you are? It's such great lighting right now."

"No bother." Brogan waved her on.

"Oh no, put your hands back as they were. Yes, like that." Kira scrambled for her camera and fired off shot after shot before Brogan stiffened up and started trying to pose for her. Within moments he was giving her a cheeky grin, and she took that picture, too, because she loved his smile.

"I'll expect a cut of the sales. I don't just model for free, you know." Brogan raised an eyebrow as she crawled back into bed.

"Naturally. I wouldn't expect you to whore out your good looks for nothing."

"I'm a respectable gentleman," Brogan agreed.

Kira refrained from pointing out that a respectable gentleman wouldn't show up drunk at a woman's house at two in the morning. Instead, she said, "I'm glad you like it here. I was hoping you wouldn't just be passing through." She rolled to her side, and this time reached out to run a finger over one of his biceps. There was a noticeable jump in his pulse, and Kira bit back a grin. Not *so* unaffected by her, then.

Brogan rolled toward her, inching down so he was lying completely flat on the bed, one arm hooked under the pillow.

"I don't think I knew what I was on about when I first came here. Mainly it was to sort out Gran's house and just take a moment out of my routine. But my stay here has blossomed into something so wildly different. I don't think I would have ever anticipated how life-changing this trip would be."

"I'm happy you're staying."

"And you? You've yet to answer my question on whether you'll stay." Blue eyes bored into hers, pinning her down for an answer she still hadn't decided upon herself.

"I… I don't rightly know just yet. I'm loving working on everything we're doing for this project. And I'm beyond thrilled you've managed to help Fergal. But my life isn't… this."

"Tell me about it."

"My life?"

"Yes. Not your career assignments but the actual day-to-day. What's it like?"

Kira considered his words. People always asked about the exciting things, like famous people she met or wild animals she saw. But rarely did anyone inquire about what the actual life of a traveling photographer was like.

"It's long periods of the mundane interspersed with moments of fabulousness. A lot of the time, I'm on my computer poring over images from a shoot or editing my choices. That's done either in my hotel room or at a coffee shop. Occasionally I'll meet with friends for a drink or a meal, or join the crew for meals, depending on the level of production I'm working on. But largely, it's a lot of me working by myself. It can be lonely, but I rarely feel alone. I love what I do and I'm perfectly content being by myself for long stretches of time."

"And if you stayed here? What would that look like?"

"I... I don't rightly know. Less loneliness, I guess. I'd have to fight for my alone time, that's for sure. I don't really have a spot of my own here."

"I'll build you a studio. By Gran's house. There's a spot for it. I already measured it out."

Kira blinked at him. His eyelids were beginning to droop and a small smile hovered on his lips.

"You... are building me a photography studio?"

"Mmmhmm. Gran would've liked it. You've the prettiest eyes, Kira. Enchanting eyes. I could spend all night looking into them and still likely wouldn't be able to count all the colors. And I love your hair."

"My hair?"

"It's wild. A bit like you. Nobody can tame you, but I hope you'll let me join you on your path."

"My..." Kira smiled as Brogan reached out and slung an arm over her waist. In seconds his eyes were closed and he was snoring lightly. Kira gaped at him, trying to process all the information she'd just learned. For a man who kept his cards close to his chest, he certainly was talkative when drinking. She waited a few moments, studying the sharp angle of Brogan's jaw, his soft lips, and his hair that had grown too long. What was the hang-up here? How could he be saying things like he wanted to be with her and was building a studio for her, and yet keep her at arm's length? The man was an enigma.

Once she was certain he was fully asleep, Kira inched out from under his arm to turn off the lights of the little studio. Sliding out of her robe, she eased back into the bed and turned her back to Brogan, moving closer to him. He shifted in his sleep and automatically reached out, slinging an arm over her waist again and pulling her closer so she was spooned against him. Her heart did a happy little dance.

No longer struggling with difficult thoughts, Kira dropped into a deep and contented sleep for the first time in weeks.

When she woke in the morning, it was to Brogan blinking down at her with a look of shock on his face.

His cheeks tinged with pink. "Please tell me I didn't do anything rude last night."

"No, not at all. You were a perfect gentleman," Kira promised, blinking the sleep from her eyes. He looked disgruntled, with rumpled hair and a confused expression on his face. She wanted to reach out and hug him and soothe the angst away.

"Kira. I can't begin to express – my deepest apologies…" Brogan trailed off as she put a finger to his lips.

"Do not apologize. I liked that you came to my doorstep when you were drunk."

"I highly doubt you enjoyed a middle-of-the-night visit."

"But I did. You were charming and absolutely

adorable. I'm glad that I was on your mind in the middle of the night."

"You are?"

"Yes. Brogan... you have to know that I like you."

"I like you too, Kira," Brogan said. He sat up, running a hand through his hair.

The man was absolutely maddening, Kira decided. She'd just professed she liked him, and here he was brushing it off like it was nothing. Gracie's words came back to her. She supposed it was time to take things into her own hands.

"If that's the case, I would like to ask you on a proper date. My treat."

Brogan looked at her as though she'd just spit in his face. "Excuse me?"

"Erm... I didn't realize the idea would be so repulsive to you." Annoyed, Kira launched herself out of bed, not caring that she was wearing only a tank top and underwear. This was what happened when she tried to date, Kira thought as she measured out the coffee. It all came back to bite her in the arse.

"I didn't... I'm not saying..." Brogan groaned and flopped back on the bed.

Turning, she put her hands on her hips and watched while he ran his hands over his face. "What are you saying, then?"

"Listen, Kira." Brogan stood up and walked to her, but paused when his eyes caught on her purple silk underwear. Distracted, he forgot to speak.

"Yes? This is the part where you tell me no and you just want to be friends, right? I'll save you the trouble.

We're friends. Go on then. Have a good day. I have to get ready for work."

"No, wait, Kira, please. Just listen." Brogan's hands landed on her shoulders and turned her gently around again so she stared mulishly at his chest.

"Go on."

"Look at me." Kira lifted sulky eyes to his. "I'm the one who's supposed to be asking *you* on a proper date. Not the other way around."

"Bollocks. Women can ask men on dates."

"I understand that. I'm not saying you don't have that right. But I'm insisting that you let me ask you on a proper date. It's not for you to be doing."

"Have I affronted your manhood?"

"A bit."

"Fine, then. Go on."

Brogan blanched. "Go on? Like… right now?"

"See? If you were excited about asking me on a date, you'd have done it by now. It's fine, Brogan. We can be friends."

"I just… I'm at war with myself, okay? This has nothing to do with you or your desirability, and everything to do with my own insecurities. I don't know if I should even start this dance when I'm not sure you're going to want to keep dancing with me once it's all over."

Kira worked to follow his fumbling logic. It sounded like he was nervous she'd give up on him quickly.

"Isn't that any dating, though? You never know how it's going to turn out. So you have to take a risk at some point, don't you?"

"But what if it goes wrong? And we still have to work

together? I don't want to lose you on this project. You're such a strong asset for the team."

"I am, aren't I?" Kira beamed up at him. "All right, if it's assurances you want… I promise if this doesn't work out – and mind you, I'm literally only asking for one date – that I will still work on the nature center and we will figure out how to still be friends."

"If that's the case, then… Kira, will you do the honor of joining me for a proper date?"

"I'll think about it." Kira sniffed and turned away. Then she let out a whooshing laugh as Brogan picked her up and tossed her onto the bed. "Brogan!"

"Enough sass out of you. Is that a yes or a no?"

"Yes, Brogan, I will go on a date with you."

"I'll message you details later, once my head stops pounding and I can plan a proper date. Don't get all moody and weird on me if you don't hear from me for a bit. I'll likely be face down in my pillows moaning about my poor life choices."

"You were quite pleased with yourself last night. A lads' night and you beat Liam at darts."

"I did! That's right. Already I'm feeling better." Brogan stopped by her door. "Thank you for your hospitality. I will see you for our date… soon."

"You're welcome…" But Kira was speaking to empty space.

She grinned as she heard Brogan clatter down the steps. Pulling a pillow over her head, she squealed into it.

Now, to work on convincing Brogan that they had more than one date in their future.

CHAPTER 20

*K*ira spent the next two days too revved up to sit still. Deciding to make use of her abundance of nerves, she'd sweetly cajoled Mr. Murphy into letting her take his portrait. She ended up photographing in and outside of Gallagher's while she was at it, even catching a few shots of Cait when the woman wasn't canny enough to turn away from her camera. She'd spent much of the previous night selecting her very favorites and now waited on pins and needles for the images to print.

While the gallery projected elegant small-town charm, it still had many modern amenities tucked away in the back room. Morgan had seen fit to add a printing room to the back, and had installed high-end printers for different sized reproductions. It had been an investment up front, but the prints they'd sold since had more than justified the expense. Kira was grateful she didn't have to seek out a professional printer for this job, as she was itching to see how her prints would look on the wall. Morgan had supplied her with frames and mats at Kira's request; she had asked nothing more, for she was used to working with moody artists.

Pleased that Morgan hadn't pushed her for details until she was ready, Kira moved to the worktable where she'd stacked the mats she wanted to use.

She'd decided to start with five images only – a selection of Grace's Cove through her eyes. She hoped they would elicit the same warm response in others as they had in her when she'd taken the photos. The printer finished the first of her prints and, setting aside three frames that would be for gifts, Kira got to work. It had been a while, she mused, since she'd been in the business of printing and framing her own work. She was so used to seeing her work in digital form only, or in a magazine, that she rarely thought about seeing it in other mediums.

Now, as she held up the first photo of Mr. Murphy, a wide smile spread across her face.

"Just look at him," Kira whispered. He was smiling, laughing at someone's banter, looking across the bar instead of directly at the camera. She'd taken the shot in black and white, so that the lines creasing his face stood out in dark relief against his skin. Behind him, a soft ray of light filtered through the window, creating a sort of halo around him, while the metal of the beer taps gleamed in the glow. He looked like every Irish grandpa she'd ever known, with a cheerful smile, a newsboy cap, and a willingness to tell a story. Nobody could look at this picture and not smile, Kira thought, and bent to mat a smaller version of the same picture as a gift for Mr. Murphy – or, more likely, for Cait. Kira knew he would probably refuse the photo, and she hoped Cait would find a spot on the wall at Gallagher's for it.

Next up, Kira framed a photo she'd taken of Gallagher's front door and window. This one she'd done in color, for Ireland was known for its brightly colored pubs, and Gallagher's was no different. With its graceful arched door, a cheerful window box full of flowers, and dark wrought-iron hinges, it invoked the days of old while also beckoning one closer. Everyone who saw the photo would want to go to this pub, Kira thought. It seemed to invite the viewer to step inside and stay for a while.

The third photo had Kira smiling once more. This one was of Cait, a smile on her face and fire in her eyes as she shot off a comment to one of her regulars while she poured a pint of Guinness. Pint-sized herself, Cait's confidence and complete command of her environment shone through in the photo. Oh, she'd be annoyed that Kira had stolen a photo of her, but Kira didn't care. She was stunning, a beautiful woman in full power of herself and her business.

Finally, Kira looked at the last two photos she wanted to sell. Both were from the hills that occupied a special place in heart. The first was of Fergal and Heather, their little paws hooked around each other as they floated in blissful sleep on the surface of the still pond. Reflected in the water were the hills behind, and the few clouds that dotted an otherwise blue sky. She'd been grateful to capture the moment, and had already had hundreds of inquiries about purchasing the image. Kira could understand why – just looking at it made her want to cuddle up with someone she loved.

The next image was of Brogan's gran's cottage. Or,

well, Brogan's cottage. She'd snuck to the cottage the same day she'd gotten the photograph of Fergal and Heather, and had crouched low to get the right angle for the photo. The clouds had been dark in the sky, and she'd waited until they moved just a bit and sun had pierced through, highlighting the cream stone cottage with the cheerful red front door. Behind it, the sea was a moody deep blue, reflecting the incoming inclement weather, and the field was a brilliant green against the cottage. Pleased with her work, Kira hummed as she finished matting and framing the photos.

Finally, she picked up an image that she'd printed just for her. She'd printed it small, the size of her hand, for it was something she wanted to keep in her journal. The picture made her heart twinge in an odd way. Her breath hitched in her chest a moment as she studied Brogan lying against her pink sheets, his muscular arms crossed and a relaxed look in his eye. If she didn't know better, it would have looked like a man sated by a recent round of love-making, comfortable in his woman's bed, looking at her with love in his eyes. Turning it over, she slid it into her journal, then put the journal into her knapsack before looking back at the table.

"Knock knock," Morgan said from the doorway.

"Come look. Tell me what you think. The frames you gave me are fantastic."

"They are," Morgan agreed, stepping forward briskly. "Locally sourced wood from old barns."

"They work." Kira pursed her lips as she studied the pictures.

"Kira… these are divine. We'll be sold out of them the

first day, I'm certain of it. You'll need to make back-up prints before we even bring them to the floor."

"You think?" Pleasure bloomed through her.

"Absolutely. This is exactly what we've been missing at the gallery. Photographs speak to a different audience. It'll round out the gallery's offerings, and they'll be easy to sell in smaller prints or as postcards. Well done, you."

"Thank you. I'm not sure what to price them at."

"I'll take care of that. You'll be compensated fairly." A sharp look came into Morgan's eyes, and Kira held up her hands and laughed.

"I trust you. Don't get your negotiating face on."

Morgan smiled. "Sorry, habit."

"I'm going to run these three over to Gallagher's. I'd like to gift them to Cait and Mr. Murphy. You can take the costs from my first sales, if you'd like."

"Nonsense. They're family. Go on, then. They'll get a kick out of these. Well, Mr. Murphy will. Cait will kick up a fuss, but secretly she'll be pleased with her photo."

"I figured as much. Which is why I didn't tell her I was taking it."

"Smart. Bossy woman."

"Much like you," Kira called, then laughed at Morgan's unladylike curse that followed her through the door. She set the photographs down long enough to tug on a light canvas jacket and grab her purse. Then, checking to make sure no rain was coming down outside, she bustled a few blocks over to the pub. Even though it was mid-afternoon, she could still hear voices drifting from the door, which had been propped open to encourage the warmish breeze inside.

"There's a beautiful lass to warm an old man's cold heart," Mr. Murphy called to her from his perch at the corner of the bar.

"And there's nothing like a kiss from a handsome lad to warm a wicked woman's heart," Kira countered. She planted a smacking kiss on Mr. Murphy's cheek.

"The best women are the wicked ones," Mr. Murphy concurred.

"Hiya, Kira. Can I get you anything?" Cait called from the other end of the bar where she washed glasses.

"A half-pint of cider will do. And your lovely presence for a wee chat, of course."

"I'll be with you shortly."

"How's the new nature center coming about?" Mr. Murphy asked. "I heard Dylan talking about arranging a shuttle once a week so any of the seniors who are interested can be driven from the community center out to the nature center once it's open. Maybe we won't be hiking any trails, but I hear there'll be some lovely tables to sit at."

"There will be. You can spend time in the hills and enjoy nature without having to go for a hike. Brogan is looking to welcome everyone – young, old, those with impairments. He's been thoughtful in his design."

"That's a good lad. I like him. We had lunch the other day."

"Did you?"

"We did. He's the way of his gran, he does. I remember her being a lovely and gracious woman. It seems the apple doesn't fall far from the tree with that one."

"Who's this now?" Cait said, stopping before them and sliding Kira's cider to her.

"The lad Brogan. I enjoyed talking to him. He didn't try to rush through my stories or talk over me. A patient sort. Kind eyes."

"I like him too," Cait said, her eyes finding Kira's. "He's worth your time."

"Is that how it is, then?" Mr. Murphy's eyes sharpened with interest. He did love a good gossip, that one, Kira thought, and decided to distract them.

"I've presents for you both," Kira said as she pulled the frames out of her tote and laid them on the bar. She'd wrapped them in a stiff parchment paper, and a sweet little bow the gallery provided.

"Are these your photos of Mr. Murphy? I can't wait to see." Cait leaned over to grab one.

"Aye, this one is Mr. Murphy's. And these two are for you, actually." Kira pointed to two of the frames.

"For me? Whatever for?" Cait murmured.

"Go on, then. Open."

"You first, Mr. Murphy," Cait said. She crossed her arms over her chest and waited as Mr. Murphy carefully picked at the tape and unfolded the paper. When his eyes landed on the picture, he sat in silence, not saying a word.

"I'm sorry… is it… do you not…" Kira looked at Cait, aghast, and then back to Mr. Murphy. His hands trembled as he held the photo. Then he looked up, tears rimming his eyes.

"It's perfect, Kira. It's exactly how I want to be remembered. As everyone's friend."

"That's exactly it, Mr. Murphy. That's the feeling I wanted to get across."

"You've done a marvelous job. I'm so proud of you." Mr. Murphy laid the photograph gently on the bar and put out his arms to pull her into a hug. He smelled like pipe tobacco and cedar, and Kira blinked, surprised to feel her own tears about to start up.

"Oh, then, you're going to get me going now too. Kira, this is marvelous. I demand a print for the pub." Kira looked up to see Cait dash the back of her hand across her eyes.

"Well, we're a lovely lot, aren't we?" Kira laughed as they all sniffled and wiped their eyes.

"Cait, you take this picture. Put it up and then when I'm gone, I'll always have a place in the pub," Mr. Murphy insisted.

"Don't talk like that, Mr. Murphy. You've years on you yet."

"Time is a fickle mistress. Please?"

"It would be my honor to have your portrait here. You can help me pick the perfect spot."

"Go on and open yours. I'm dying to see."

Kira watched Cait carefully as she pried the paper off and turned the photo over. A flash of embarrassment crossed her face, then a look of pride replaced it.

"You weren't supposed to be taking photos of me," Cait said lightly, sending Kira a warning look.

"Aye, I know. But you're a brilliant subject."

"Let me see then." Mr. Murphy took the print from Cait before she could object.

"You nimble old coot," Cait muttered.

"You foul-mouthed harpy," Mr. Murphy shot back. They grinned at each other in companionable ease.

"Do you not like it?" Kira worried.

"While I'm fairly partial to my portrait, I'll have to concede defeat. This is the best portrait I've seen. Just look at you, Cait! All fire and brimstone for the devil in you, and all woman and beauty for the angel in you. It's a fine portrait you've done, Kira."

"It's not half bad," Cait sniffed.

"I'll take it," Kira decided.

"You put that picture up next to mine. It's the perfect pairing. Me one side of the bar and you cracking off on the other side," Mr. Murphy insisted.

Cait shook her head. "I don't know…"

"You don't get my portrait if you don't put yours up."

"Stubborn arse," Cait muttered.

"Beautiful, powerful Cait – let yourself be celebrated," Mr. Murphy said.

Cait's shoulders slumped. "You do me in, Kira. This is lovely."

"Good, I'm glad you like it. And I think the both of you will agree on the last one."

Sure enough, they oohed and ahhed over the photograph of the front of Gallagher's, with Cait insisting she order a run of prints that customers could buy. They even discussed making coasters of the image, a thought which both delighted Kira and made her wrinkle her nose in disgust as it seemed so commercial to her. When her phone buzzed, she glanced at it to see a text from Brogan.

I'd like to formally invite you on a date tomorrow afternoon, if you are free. I'll pick you up at 3:00?

3:00 for a date?

Yes, that's when I can get away from my meetings. Come hungry. I mean… if you'll join me, that is.

I look forward to it.

"And who has brought that little smile to your face?" Cait demanded.

"You know who." Kira glared at her.

"I like him," Cait said, holding her eyes. "I really like him. He's steady. He'd be good for you, I think, if you'll let him in."

"I've been trying. The man is tricky to pin down."

"He needs to trust that you won't up and leave," Cait said. Mr. Murphy wisely stayed silent, his eyes darting between the two as he followed their conversation.

"I can't promise that, Cait. My career is centered on traveling around the world."

"Your career is here." Cait tapped the photo of Mr. Murphy. "You don't need to go everywhere else to find inspiration."

"It's not that simple."

"It can be. You have choices to make." With that, Cait swept up her photos and ducked underneath the passthrough at the end of the bar to disappear into her back office.

"She makes it sound so easy," Kira muttered into her cider.

"Nothing in life is easy. But she's right, it comes down to choices. I'll say this: Brogan's a nice lad. Boy needs family. You need to decide if you can be that for him before you go any further."

Kira blew out a breath.

"That's a lot of pressure on a first date."

"That's what makes it matter."

———

ONCE KIRA HAD LEFT the pub, Cait looked around at the regulars. Reaching under the bar, she hauled out a large leatherbound ledger.

"I'm opening bets on when Kira and Brogan get together," Cait called out.

Shouts broke out as everyone lined up to place their bets.

Kira better get used to living in a small town again, Cait thought with a smile. She licked her pencil and glared at Mr. Murphy. "I've a mind to keep you out of this one. You're starting to win too many."

"Now, have a heart, Cait…"

CHAPTER 21

*B*rogan had instructed her to wear clothes for the
outdoors, so Kira was left to work on a cute
date outfit that would also protect her from any elements.
So much for the sexy low-cut top she'd planned to wear,
Kira thought, and tossed that to the side. Instead, she
pulled on skinny jeans and a slouchy purple sweater, and
hung bright turquoise drops at her ears. Remembering his
comment about how he liked her hair wild, Kira ran her
hands through her curls and tousled them so that they
swung freely down her back. She used a light hand with
her makeup, and when she was done, she grabbed her coat,
her camera, and her purse. She ran down her steps just as
Brogan pulled into the little alleyway behind the gallery.
She'd told him to come there instead of out front, unless he
wanted the whole town to start talking.

Nerves jittered in her stomach as Brogan got out of the
car and smiled lazily at her.

"You look pretty."

"Thank you," Kira said. Brogan delighted her by

bending over to brush a soft kiss across her lips. His scent – soap and a hint of the outdoors – drifted over her.

"You're supposed to tell me I look handsome too," Brogan said as he rounded the car to hold the door for her.

"Well, now that you mention it…" Kira teased as she slid into the passenger's seat. She waited until Brogan got into the driver's seat. "You look very nice today, Brogan."

"Nice is for sissies," Brogan grumbled, shocking a laugh from Kira.

"You look like a bold warrior ready to fight for my honor," Kira promised him. Brogan slid her a look. He did look handsome, Kira thought as they left the village and headed for the narrow road that wound through the cliffs toward the cove. He had on faded grey canvas pants, a thick heather grey sweater, and his sturdy hiking boots. Certainly not dressed like a sissy, though Kira kind of wished he'd put his glasses on so she could sigh over them.

"How have you been since I last showed up at your doorstep?" Brogan asked.

"I've been well, thank you. Busy working, actually. On my own prints."

"Is that right?"

Kira told him about what she'd been up to and he rewarded her with a pleased smile.

"I can't wait to see them. Especially the otter one. It sounds like you'll have to put that one up at the nature center."

"It's absolutely darling," Kira promised him. "Before I came back here, I had no idea otters cuddled in the water when they slept. I mean, it just kills me."

"It's really cute. I've seen them do it a couple of times now. One time they woke up and came to the side of the pond, and I felt like I'd kicked a puppy or something. They seemed happy to see me – or maybe it was the fish I had – but I hated to interrupt their peaceful moment."

"I'm sure they have plenty of them. They're out there all day long with little disturbance."

"I suppose. I still felt like I'd walked in on a special moment or something."

"How are things going with the planning of the center?"

"Amazingly well, actually." Brogan slowed as they approached a particularly tight curve in the road. "With the help of Dylan and Liam, things are moving way faster than I could have ever imagined."

Kira desperately wanted to ask him about the studio he had claimed he was building for her, but bit her words back. All in good time, she reminded herself.

"Are we going to see the otters then?" Kira asked. Brogan had driven past the cove and up the winding road that led toward the otters, his land, and his gran's cottage. Her heart skipped a beat, wondering if he was taking her to his home instead.

"I hadn't planned on it, but we're close. Do you want to pop by and see them?"

"Do we have time?"

"Of course," Brogan promised, pulling the car to the side at the trailhead. "The rest of my day is all yours."

And night, Kira silently hoped.

It was a quick hike from where Brogan had stopped the

car. As they approached, a nervous feeling began creeping over Kira, and she couldn't shake it.

"Brogan. Be careful... I don't know. I feel like something bad is happening."

"What's wrong?" Brogan stopped instantly and turned to her. "Do we need to go back?"

Kira closed her eyes and listened with her senses. "No, it's at the pond. Hurry!"

Together they raced the rest of the way up the hill. They rounded the cusp of the hill in time to see a large man holding Fergal by the scruff of his neck, with a knife in his free hand.

Before Kira could shout, Brogan was on him. She'd never seen someone move so fast before, she was sure of it. Kira gasped as Fergal was flung to the side, his little furry body lofting through the air and landing with a hard splash in the water. She rushed to the side of the pond and waded in, not caring about getting wet.

"Fergal," Kira whispered, reaching for the otter who floated naturally on the surface. She picked him up gently and was relieved when his eyes blinked open.

Friend. Mean man.

"Yes, mean man. Are you hurt?"

No. Where's Heather?

Kira craned her neck while she cradled Fergal, and caught a flash of movement in the corner of the pond.

"She's just over there. Hiding."

Put me down. I have to go to her.

"Is she hurt?"

No. He got me first. Destroyed my den.

"We'll build you a new one." Kira gently put Fergal

back in the water, then turned as a sickening crunching sound met her ears. The men had squared off, and Kira gasped at the blood she saw running down Brogan's face.

Her stomach twisted as the man landed a punch in Brogan's gut, but he barely flinched. Instead, he caught the other man's chin with a stiff uppercut that had the stranger staggering backward. Racing from the pond, Kira crept up behind the man and delivered a solid kick between his legs. A squeal of pain left the man's lips, and as he doubled over, Brogan knocked him unconscious with one more punch. He crumpled like a sack of potatoes.

A furry streak raced from the water, and Kira gasped as Fergal sank his teeth into the man's leg. Heather followed suit, applying her sharp teeth to the man's groin.

"Fergal! It's okay, we've got it. Thank you for helping."

Bloody arse.

"Yes, he's an arse. Heather, are you all right?"

Yes.

Brogan had dropped to the ground and cradled his head in his hands. Kneeling beside him, Kira pulled his hands away and gasped at the amount of blood that poured down his face.

"Brogan, are you okay?"

"I think so. His ring caught me, I think. I don't know. It's a bit blurry. I reckon I was acting on adrenaline."

"You were fierce. Just – here, put pressure on it." Kira handed him her scarf and pressed it to his head. "I'm going to call Gracie. I saw her car at her cottage."

"I don't think a tonic's going to do much. I think I need stitches."

"Just… trust me." Kira pulled out her phone and called Grace three times before she picked up.

"What now? I'm in the middle of –"

"Brogan's hurt. We're at the pond. There was an attack. Have Dylan call the Gardaí, and I need you to come heal him."

"I'll be there as soon as I can. Keep pressure on anything bleeding."

"I will."

Kira tucked the phone into her back pocket and pressed her hands back to Brogan's skull. His hands dropped to his side, and he seemed to be struggling to breathe.

"Where else does it hurt?"

"My side. I think. I might have. Broken my ribs."

Tears sprang to Kira's eyes. "I can't believe this happened."

Construction man.

"It was? Oh no," Kira said, looking down at Fergal. He had crept closer, Heather at his side.

"What?"

"They say it was a construction man."

"Makes sense. He's a brute."

"Mad he lost a job, likely."

The otters crept closer, then, seeming to come to their own decision, they climbed lightly into Brogan's lap and curled up into two little balls. Brogan's hands came up and he gently cradled his arms around them.

"I'm so sorry," Brogan told them.

Not your fault.

"They say it's not your fault."

"It is, though. If I hadn't cut off the construction, they wouldn't have been hurt."

Our pond would've been gone.

"They say they still would've been hurt. Their home would've been gone. Plus, Fergal told me neither of them are actually injured. He was just a little stunned from being thrown."

"I'm glad they're safe." Brogan's head dropped to his chest.

"Stay with me, buddy. Gracie will be here soon."

Brogan cuddled the otters closer; Kira was grateful for their warmth as his body began to shake. Shock was setting in, and she had nothing for him other than her body heat. She was saved from wondering what to do next by a shout from across the pond.

Gracie and Dylan ran over the hill, and Kira let out a sigh of relief.

"They're friends," Kira promised as the otters jumped in Brogan's lap. "They're coming to help Brogan."

The otters stood their ground, which showed just how much trust they had in Kira – especially after the attack they'd just experienced.

"Where is he hurt?" Gracie skidded to a halt and lowered to her knees, dropping the sack she'd brought with her. "Cute otters."

"I'll just make certain this lad isn't a problem anymore," Dylan said, rolling the unconscious man over and tying his wrists together.

"Is he breathing?" Gracie called, running her hands over Brogan's body.

"Aye. He'll keep. See to Brogan."

"He mentioned his ribs, and obviously, he's gushing blood from his head. Not sure where else yet."

"Let me do a body scan and then I'll get to work. Let's lay him back and get something soft under his head."

"My jacket." Kira took off her jacket and balled it up. Crouching, she made a pillow for Brogan, then turned to the otters. "Guys, my friend Gracie here is going to work to heal Brogan. There's some magick involved, so you'll be safest if you go back to the pond and give her some room."

Friend. Save Brogan.

"Yes, she'll take care of him. I promise."

The otters scampered off, sliding back into the water and moving a safe distance away. Kira and Dylan quickly stretched a mumbling Brogan out while Gracie went to work.

"He's got massive bruising to his chest and his gut, perhaps some internal bleeding, and I think a concussion," Gracie said, her eyes still closed as her hands flew over Brogan. "I'm going to start now before anything gets worse."

Knowing that Gracie needed all of her attention to work her healing magicks, Kira kept silent and lifted her own silent prayer to the goddess that Brogan would be okay. The internal bleeding was deeply concerning for her.

Twenty tense minutes later, a cloud of darkness zipped from Gracie and exploded in the dirt on the other side of the pond. Gracie looked up, sweat pouring off her brow, her eyes tired but relieved.

"He's fine now. Though I do recommend a good rest."

"That's it? He doesn't need to go into hospital or anything?"

"Do you think I'd be lying to you, then?" Gracie glared at her as more noise greeted them from across the pond.

"That's the Gardaí; I'll go greet them," Dylan said.

"I'm just worried," Kira said, still trembling from the adrenaline that coursed through her.

"I know it. We'll get him home and you can nurse him back to health. But he really should be fine – just tired. I promise."

"Thank you. It's a miracle gift you have, that's the truth of it."

"We all have our strengths," Gracie said, and stood. Whether she kicked the man lying on the ground as she went past was something Kira would never tell.

"Hey." Kira smiled down at Brogan, who was blinking wearily up at her. "Let's get you home."

"What... how am I?"

"Gracie healed you."

"Is that right? She's a good woman, that one."

"Aye, she is. Let's get you out of here."

"We'll give our statement to the police first," Brogan sat up, then stood. Though he was shaky at first, he seemed to recover quickly. Kira jumped up and threaded her arm through his, just in case, and they headed over to give the police their statements.

"I want to stay until he's gone," Brogan said, nodding to where the intruder had regained consciousness.

"That's fair. But then we're getting you home."

"I do feel a bit tired," Brogan admitted.

He was white as a ghost and covered with blood, but

Kira refrained from pointing that out. They waited in silence until the pond area cleared.

"Good to go?"

"Just a moment." Brogan went to the edge of the pond near what was left of Fergal's Fortress. Seeing that the coast was clear, the otters came out of the brushes and swam to Brogan. "I'm so sorry about this. I'll try to keep you protected, I promise."

"Gracie is coming back to magick it."

Brogan looked at her. "Magick what?"

"This area. A perimeter of protection. Nobody with nefarious intentions will be able to get through."

"Did I mention she's a good woman?"

"You did, at that."

Friend. Take care of him.

"I will. He's worried about you both."

We're worried about him.

"I'll take him home and promise to take care of him. We'll come back to see you when he's rested."

Thank you.

"I'm under strict orders from the otters and Gracie to take you home. Enough dawdling. Let's go, my warrior."

"Ha – I guess I did need to be a warrior today." Brogan stood and accepted her arm, and they began the trek down to the car.

"You did. And you were magnificent."

"I do what I can to impress the ladies."

"Mmmhmm," Kira said, holding him upright as he stumbled over a few rocks. No need to crush his ego now. "You're a fierce one, you are, Brogan."

"I'll take it."

CHAPTER 22

"*I* really don't think I need to lie down," Brogan protested as she pushed him toward the bedroom tucked in the back of his cottage.

"Doctor's orders."

"But…"

"Now is really not the time to push me, Brogan, or you're going to learn about my temper really quick."

"What if I want to see your temper?" Brogan argued.

Kira sighed, a bone-deep exhaustion coursing through her now that the danger had passed. "Please?"

"Fine. But only since you've asked nicely. I made you dinner, by the way. But it's in the car. If you're hungry. Ah, hell, I'm doing a bloody awful job of this wooing thing." Brogan sighed and sat on the edge of the bed.

It was a cheerful room, with two wide windows that offered a pretty sea view, worn wood beams running across the ceilings, and a cheerful coverlet done up in soothing green and blue tones.

"Compromise? I'll get the food and we can eat in here."

"I can get –" Brogan broke off at her glare. Sighing, he bent to take his shoes off. Heading back outside, Kira retrieved the hamper, hooked it on her arm, and returned to the bedroom. As she'd anticipated, Brogan was almost asleep.

"Kira, come sit with me."

"I… all right then. Let me just put this down." Kira was too tired to argue. The events of the day, coupled with the lack of sleep from her last two days of manic work, came crashing into her. She set the hamper down near the bed and bent to untie her shoes. Feeling dizzy, she reached her hand out to steady herself on the bed.

"Are you hurt?"

"I think I'm just… I'm cold and wet and scared and…" Kira's voice hitched.

"Take off your clothes. I promise not to look, if you don't want me to. Here…" Brogan pulled the coverlet up. "Wrap yourself in this if you need to."

Too tired to argue, her nerves frayed, Kira pulled off her soggy jeans and sweater. She climbed into bed with Brogan, not caring that he got an eyeful of her in her underwear. She'd chosen a pretty set, a deep silky red lined in black lace, but at the time, she'd thought they'd be in a very different frame of mind when they ended up in bed together.

"Come here," Brogan said, pulling the covers up so she could slide over and into his arms.

"I shouldn't be so close to you. Your ribs."

"Do you see even a bruise on me? Gracie did a bang-up job of healing me."

"You still have blood on you," Kira said, reaching up to rub at a spot on his neck.

"We'll wash it off later. Just close your eyes for a moment, Kira. Let it all slide away. I've got you, love."

Kira wasn't sure who fell asleep faster, but exhaustion claimed her as she burrowed into his warmth. Together, cocooned beneath the blankets, they healed their trauma as the day slipped into night.

Hours later, Kira blinked awake. She was comfortable in the way that only happens after a really excellent sleep. The desire to not move, to stay exactly where she was, warred with her need for the toilet. Moving gently so as not to wake Brogan, she slid from the blankets and tiptoed across to the bathroom. Making short use of the toilet, she studied herself in the mirror after. Dark circles smudged her eyes, but otherwise, she looked fine. Sleepy, but the color had returned to her face.

Tiptoeing back, Kira bent to try and find her clothes in the darkness when a hand reached out and grabbed her.

"Brogan!" Kira gasped, his touch shocking her.

"Get back in bed," Brogan demanded. When she didn't move, he simply leaned over and hauled her back underneath the covers with him.

"Brogan, I should probably go."

Kira blinked as a soft light was switched on, then Brogan rolled back to face her. She studied him, looking for any signs of injury. Aside from some dried blood still on his face, he looked just fine.

"You are going nowhere. Let me use the bathroom and

wash some of this blood off." Brogan rolled off the bed, and Kira gaped at him as he bent and scooped her clothes up and took them to the bathroom with him. So much for leaving, Kira thought; apparently, she was being held hostage in this bed. Not that it was a particularly bad spot to be in, she mused, snuggling beneath the covers more. She heard the shower come on and her stomach grumbled. Maybe she could just sneak a peek in the hamper...

Brogan came out with a towel wrapped loosely around his waist, and another hunger took over Kira's thoughts. Her mouth went dry as he came to the edge of the bed, his blue eyes radiating an icy heat as he looked down at her.

"I had a very nice date planned for you. A proper date where I was going to wine and dine you. Seduce you slowly," Brogan said in a matter-of-fact tone. "I was going to impress you with my cooking skills. Woo you with my excellent conversation. Make you laugh with my impeccable sense of humor and precise comedic timing."

"Is that right?" Kira's pulse picked up.

"I would like the record to reflect that *was* my plan."

"So noted."

"However, I've also learned that it's important to be able to adapt to unexpected roadblocks or diversions in one's plans."

"Right." Kira's mouth went dry as Brogan dropped his towel.

"I'm modifying the plan. We're doing this backwards now. I'll feed you after."

Brogan dove into the bed, startling Kira into a half-laugh, half-squeal as he pounced on her. His mouth closed on hers, and an instant heat shot through her. She moaned

as his lips pressed hot against hers. Arching her back, she
wrapped her arms around his broad shoulders, loving the
play of muscle that rippled under her arms as he shifted,
angling himself over her. Kira moaned as he deepened the
kiss, finding her tongue with his, playing out an elaborate
dance as he teased her.

Kira shuddered as Brogan broke the kiss. He pulled
back to run a finger down the lacy strap of her bra to the
red silk that covered her breast.

"Have I told you how beautiful I think you are?"

"You may have mentioned it." Kira gasped as he found
her nipple with his mouth, wetting the silk that covered it
and teasing it into a hard little nub.

"Perfection," Brogan breathed against her breast. "I've
been aching for you for weeks. I want to go slowly with
you and savor every inch of you. But I'm not sure how
long I'll last."

"Go slow later," Kira panted as he continued to toy
with her breast, his mouth sending heat flashing through
her. She moaned as his hand slid across her skin, down her
side, and cupped the soft flesh of her thigh. His hands were
everywhere, and she could barely think as he stroked her,
leaving no part of her untouched. It was like he was examining her, learning where her sensitive spots were, and
taking notes in a painstakingly methodical manner. For a
man who'd said he wouldn't be able to take it slowly, Kira
desperately wondered what him actually taking his time
would be like. Her entire body burned for him, and liquid
heat pooled low inside her.

"You're sensitive here," Brogan said, his mouth at the
delicate skin of her thigh behind her knee. He blew softly

on her skin and Kira's leg jerked in response, goosebumps skimming across her skin.

"Yes... I... oh, Brogan. I need you."

"Let me tend to you, my love," Brogan said, kissing his way up her thigh, the soft heat of his mouth driving Kira nearly to the brink. When his mouth found her panties, Kira shivered as he leveled himself up on muscular arms and slowly slid one lace strap down her thigh. "Open for me, Kira, that's a love."

Kira moved her legs open, allowing Brogan to tug her silky panties off. She shivered as he settled between her legs and ran a finger over her most sensitive spot. Kira bucked against his hand, her nerve endings stretching, aching for more from him.

"Shhh. I've got you, Kira. Let go." Brogan's mouth came hot to hers as he slid a finger slickly inside her, shocking her with the movement. She moaned against his tongue as a second finger joined the first, and he expertly sent her careening right over the cliff into such exquisite waves of pleasure that Kira gasped against his mouth, all but riding his hand, his tongue capturing her cries.

Kira lay back, spent, her body shivering in the aftermath. She smiled up at Brogan as he protected himself and then positioned himself once again between her legs.

"You're all I've thought about since the day I met you, Kira. You're incredible. I've never known a soul as magickal as yours," Brogan said, his eyes haunted with lust and something more.

"Brogan... I'm yours. Don't you know that?" Kira whispered against his mouth and then arched as he entered her in one smooth motion. She clenched around him, pulling him tighter to her, wanting every bit of him that he would give. Desperate for each other, lost in the moment, they succumbed to their pleasure as the wave crashed over them both, pulling them under.

Moments later – or hours; it was hard to say, really – Kira blinked up at the wood beams crossing the ceiling. Her body felt loose and loved, and she was looking forward to what their next round would be like, when Brogan slowed it down even further. If it was anything like doing business with him, she suspected he would take it step by erotic step.

"Next phase of the plan," Brogan said, his voice muffled in the pillow as he rolled to the side and leaned over the bed. Scooping up the hamper, he plopped it on the bed. "We'll have a picnic right here."

"A picnic in bed? How scandalous for a first date." Kira laughed at him, holding her hand to her mouth in pretend shock.

"Well, Kira, something you should know about me is that I like to live on the edge. I'm a bit of a brawler, you know." Brogan tried a rakish look for her, raising an eyebrow and turning a stern face in her direction.

"Of course. You, sir, are a rebel. One I'm lucky enough to have snagged for the night," Kira said, laughing.

Brogan's hands stilled as he unpacked the basket. "Is it just for the night then?"

He kept his tone light, but Kira could feel the shift in his mood instantly. Reaching out, she ran a hand down his arm.

"I hope not. Not for me, it isn't," she said softly.

"It's not for me, either." Brogan turned, spearing her

with a look so hot she was surprised it didn't burn her skin. "I want more than a night with you, Kira. I want…"

"What do you want?"

"It's too much to speak of for a first date. Right now, I want to feed you." A stubborn look crossed his face and Kira knew she would be getting no more information out of him.

"Well, I know I want food. And then I want another round with you, if you're up for it." Kira kept her tone light, even though her emotions seemed to be tying themselves in knots.

"At your service, my lady."

CHAPTER 23

*a*fter hearing about the attack, which was all anyone in the village could talk about, Morgan had called Kira. After first making sure she was safe, she'd told her to take the day off from the gallery. Happy to have the day free, and luxuriating in the laziness of curling up with a handsome man, Kira leaned into Brogan and watched a wren that had perched on the windowsill outside his bedroom. She liked that the windows didn't have curtains, and that daylight flooded the room. It was a pretty spot to wake up in, seeming to invite the outdoors in. Kira itched to grab her camera and take some photos of the charming wren that tilted its head at her in inquiry.

"Yes, I'm new here," Kira whispered to the wren. "But I promise I won't disturb you. You're really darling, you know that?"

Lovely.

"Yes, you are," Kira agreed, then turned when she heard a low rumble of laughter next to her.

"Are you talking to the wren?"

"I am. I think she's wondering what's going on in here."

"She's used to me being in here alone," Brogan agreed. "Be careful. She might not want to share me."

"Day one, and I'm already competing with another bird," Kira teased.

"Never," Brogan said, turning her in his arms so that she looked up at him. "I don't play games, Kira. I would never try to make you jealous. And I can promise you I'd never step out on you."

"I... I get that about you, Brogan. I can read your aura, you know," Kira said. Her heart caught as he pulled her into a fierce hug.

"What does my aura say?"

"It's a good aura. Actually, it was the first thing I saw about you, and made me like you. It's a beautiful blue with shades of green. It shows you're very loyal and that your character is strong."

"What color is your aura?"

"We actually have similar colors, but mine has a lot of streaks of magenta and purple. That reflects my creative nature and my independent streak."

Brogan's hand trailed lightly across her back, and Kira wanted to stretch lazily underneath it or purr like a contented kitten.

"Is your independence very important to you?"

"Of course. I pride myself on being able to make my way in this world on my own. I don't ask for handouts. I'm proud of what I've built in my name."

"But that's your career. Which you absolutely should be proud of. I Googled you, you know?"

"Did you? Find anything interesting?"

"About a gazillion stunning images that took my breath away. A few gossip mags about past flings of yours as well."

Kira closed her eyes and sighed. "Jax?"

"A rock star, huh?"

"It's not as cool as it sounds." Kira tilted her head to look up at his face.

"It sounds pretty cool." Brogan's tone was light, but she wondered what hovered beneath the surface that wasn't being said.

"It's cool if you like the all-access pass he came with. Free entrance into the hottest clubs, best restaurants, meeting other famous people. It's not cool if you want an actual relationship. There was only one person Jax could be in a relationship with, and that was himself."

"You don't miss that? The lifestyle, that is? New cities and fancy restaurants?"

"I... well, sometimes I do. I love discovering new places. It feeds my soul, that's for sure. I find it inspiring, and a new place always challenges me to push the boundaries of my photography."

"I understand. Do you want some breakfast?" Brogan changed the subject lightning-quick, and Kira worried that she'd said something wrong. But there was nothing wrong with being honest, Kira reminded herself. She watched as Brogan pulled on a loose pair of sweatpants.

"I'd love some. Morgan gave me the day off. It sounds like our experience yesterday is the talk of the village. Are you feeling all right? Any soreness?"

Brogan came and stood by the bed, and executed an

awkward little dance that had her falling back to the pillows and laughing.

"Well, Gracie wasn't able to fix my poor dancing skills, but she certainly mended the rest of me. Hell of a skill to have, I have to say. I'm dying to ask her how it works."

Kira rolled out of bed and stood by him, surprised when he immediately gathered her in his arms.

"Sorry, it's been so hard for me to be near you and not be able to touch you. I'm cashing in my chips now," Brogan explained, his mouth pressed to her hair.

"You have a free pass to touch me all you'd like," Kira promised.

"I may be the luckiest man alive," Brogan decided.

"And don't you be forgetting it."

"I'd like to take you somewhere today. Where I meant to take you yesterday, actually. Will you come with me?"

"I'm yours for the day. Although, you know we'll have to go to Gallagher's later and tell everyone the story or Cait will skin us."

"Yes, I'm beginning to get used to the expectations that come with living in a small town."

"On the plus side, you'll be hailed a hero, so that'll be good for your ego."

"Me?" A delighted flush crossed Brogan's cheeks. "A hero? Isn't that something. I'm hardly a hero if I couldn't walk out of the fight. Had Gracie not arrived, I would have been in much worse shape. Gracie's the real hero."

"You still took the man down. Gracie didn't do that."

"You helped. Nice kick, by the way. Well-placed."

"I had to do something. I can't even tell you how my heart stopped when I saw Fergal fly through the air."

"Should we go visit them today? Just to check in?"

"Do you mind? I've grown ridiculously attached to the both of them." Kira stopped at the door to the bathroom.

"Of course not. I'm also very attached to them. I'm a bit jealous you can speak to them, to be honest."

"I'll be your translator."

Kira hurried through a quick shower, then dressed in the same clothes from yesterday and piled her curls on top of her head in a messy bun. There would be no use trying to comb through her hair after the energetic night they'd had before, so it was best to just keep it from knotting further.

"Coffee, toast, and some scrambled eggs. Does that suit you?" Brogan asked from where he stood at the compact stovetop in the kitchen.

"I'm easy. That sounds perfect." Kira walked around the combined kitchen and living room, studying the various knick-knacks and photos on the walls. "Oh, look. There's Fiona."

Brogan crossed to look at a photo of two women laughing in a field.

"That's my gran on the right. She was a good soul. I wish I could have spent more time here than I did. I wish she'd been my mother. Being raised here would have been good for me." Sadness laced Brogan's words.

"She looks to be a good soul. But I'm not sure you should've grown up here. Then you wouldn't be you. And I like this version of you." Kira turned and put her hand to his face, leaning up to kiss him.

"Thanks for that," Brogan said when he pulled back, a dazzled look on his face. "There's a few photos of me as a child in that album there."

"Oh, my favorite! Childhood photos are always so awkward. Can I see?"

"Sure, have a look. I'll finish with the breakfast."

Kira dropped to the table and paged through the album. She laughed at an image of a young Brogan running haphazardly through a field with a kite in hand. But her hand stilled when she found another picture of Brogan. This image of him was such a contrast to the others that she reached up and rubbed her heart, where a little ache pulsed.

Brogan was likely only ten years old in this photo, but his spirit was shadowed. His expression was sullen, his eyes defiant, as he glared out at the camera. Behind him, a woman stood with her hand on his shoulder, posing with a smile. The smile didn't reach her eyes, and it looked like the person taking the photo had interrupted a scolding.

"Ah, I was mad there. Mam had taken my book away."

"Why did she do that?"

"She told me I had to go outside and play. That I wasn't normal like other boys were."

"Oh, Brogan, I'm sorry."

Brogan just shrugged.

"Can I... do you mind if I touch it?" Kira whispered, wanting to understand the depths of Brogan's pain.

Brogan tilted his head at Kira. "What will that do?"

"I'll be able to feel this memory."

"Why would you want to? It's just unhappiness."

"So I can be understanding you better."

"I suppose that's what they mean by being vulnerable in a relationship…" Brogan sighed. "Go ahead then."

Kira reached out and slid the photo from the plastic, closing her eyes to focus on the photo and the memories that flooded her. Oh, it was much worse than he remembered, she realized. Brogan had told her he'd been scolded for reading, but it was much, much worse. Tears sprang unbidden to her eyes as she heard his mother's rant as she walked through the house, shattering plates on the floor.

You're lazy. Just like your father. Though we don't even know who he is, do we now? That man could barely get it up. Just like most men. Worthless creatures, men. All you do is complicate my life. Why don't you go out and make some actual money instead of burying your head in your books? You're useless to me. A useless, weak, poor excuse for a man. You'll never amount to anything, that's the truth of it.

Her heart cracked for the little boy who ducked his head and only wanted to read his book. This woman had such a precious soul at her disposal and had done her damndest to destroy it. If she wasn't already dead, Kira would have had a mind to pay her a very unpleasant visit.

"Well, that's a mood killer, isn't it?" Brogan said lightly as he put a plate of food in front of her. He sat down across the table from her, his face impassive.

"Brogan, I'm so sorry you lived through this. What a horrible woman. She didn't break you, though." Kira reached out with both hands and took his in her own. "She did her best, but she didn't break you. Your light still shines… oh so brilliantly. I'm so glad you're you."

"Gran helped," Brogan admitted. "It was like she worked feverishly to undo all the awful things I'd hear."

"I'm glad for it. You didn't deserve that, Brogan. You were just a child."

"I understand that. I've worked through most of it. Some of it still hits hard at moments." Brogan shrugged.

"Of course it will. Trauma doesn't just disappear in a day. Its roots go much deeper."

He quirked a smile at her. "So much for being your fierce warrior."

"Oh, Brogan. You're so much more my fierce warrior now. Not only can you take down a construction thug, but you fought the biggest battle of all – not letting someone change who you are. You stood strong through years of abuse. I'm so proud of you."

"Jeez, Kira. You're going to make a blubbering mess of me, you are," Brogan joked, but Kira could see the sheen of tears that had sprung to his eyes.

"Right, well, let's eat this scrumptious meal so you can show me your surprise then." Kira released his hands and dug into her breakfast. They ate in silence for a while, just the wren's birdsong accompanying them.

After a moment, Brogan looked up.

"Thank you for seeing me."

CHAPTER 24

"Should we check on Fergal first?" Brogan asked as they stepped outside the cottage.

It was one of those perfect first days of spring. A few puffy clouds dotted the skies and the sun felt warm and welcoming on her face.

"I'll admit, it would make me feel better."

"Me too." A sheepish grin crossed Brogan's handsome face. Impulsively, Kira reached out and took his hand.

"Amazing how those little guys have grown on us in such a short time."

"Aye, but I feel a duty to them. They live on my land – or, I suppose, I live on theirs – and I want to make sure they're protected. It just kills me how close they were to being hurt yesterday."

"But they weren't. We got there in time. Remember, Gracie magicked the area after she healed you. And she said she's going to work on more protections today. Trust me, one does not mess with Gracie when she's furious."

"That makes me feel better."

"Look!" Kira said as they rounded the bend to the pond. Fergal and Heather scampered about on the shoreline, chasing each other, their furry little bodies moving far faster than Kira would have thought possible. "What are they doing?"

"I think… oh, let's give them some privacy." Brogan laughed and tugged her away before the otters saw them.

"Spring is in the air and all that…" Kira laughed. "Oh, I'm glad they aren't traumatized by yesterday."

"They don't look to be, in my estimation."

"Oh my goddess!" Kira stopped in her tracks and looked up at Brogan.

Concern flashed in his eyes. "What?"

"Baby otters! We're going to be grandparents!" Kira did a little dance in the dirt.

"I'll admit, that does sound pretty damn cute." Brogan laughed and tugged her toward a trailhead that started to the right of his cottage.

"I'm going to have to live up here and stalk them every day. Can you imagine the photographs? In Otter News is going to explode," Kira said with a laugh.

"Do you think you'd like that? Living up here?" Brogan asked, his tone light. But Kira could feel the yearning beneath his words. Her heart screamed yes, but she needed to be honest with herself and him.

"I don't yet know. I'm still figuring out my direction, I suppose."

"That's a fair answer."

"But not the one you wanted." Kira looked up at him.

"Honesty is all I'll ever ask of you, Kira. In fact, it's vitally important to me. Growing up how I did – with someone whose emotions changed on a dime and who often went back on their word... well, I've come to value honesty more than anything else in the world. I may not always like what I hear, but I will respect you more if you are always truthful."

"I'm not a liar," Kira said, as they continued up the trail leading up the side of the hill. "And I won't hide my feelings even if I know they make someone uncomfortable – but there's a difference between being deliberately hurtful and being honest with your thoughts."

"There is. And what I'm hearing from you is that you need time."

"Time for... Brogan, we just had our first date. What are you asking exactly?" Kira's heart did a funny little shiver in her chest as she looked up at him. Was he going to ask her for more? Or tell her about the photography studio? What did he want from her? The cove said he was her forever mate. Her one true love. But did that mean she had to sacrifice everything she'd worked for to have him?

"I'm asking for your time," Brogan said, squeezing her hand.

"And that's it? Just my time?"

"Yes. Let's see where this goes. I want more time with you. And I think you need it, too, to think about what your next steps are."

Kira pushed her lip out. "Why does this feel like I'm a petulant child being told to think about my actions?"

"It's not that." Brogan laughed and bent to capture her lips with his own. "I promise it's not. I want what you're willing to give me, Kira. I'm telling you I'll wait for you to figure things out."

"And if I decide to leave?"

"I would never stop you, Kira. You have to know that. I'd no more clip a bird's wings than I would hold you back from what your heart wants."

"Thank you," Kira whispered. Her emotions were in turmoil. It felt like she needed to make a decision right this minute, but she just couldn't. She loved being with Brogan, and she believed the message that the cove had sent her. But she just couldn't fathom giving up her career. The thought of not being able to get up and go when she got a great assignment chafed at her.

"Okay, I'll have to ask you to close your eyes."

"Oh yeah?" Kira put her hands over her eyes.

"No peeking."

"Promise."

Brogan took hold of her arm and tugged her gently forward. He stopped walking and put his hands on her shoulders, turning her so that he was behind her.

"Go ahead then. You can look."

Kira gasped as she opened her eyes. Before her, the world seemed to sweep out in gentle rolling green hills until it dropped off the edge into the sea. A large rectangular plot of land had been dug up; the four corners were marked with rebar posts that had tiny little flags fluttering in the wind. Behind them, a cliff wall rose to shelter the spot.

"Is this...?"

"Yes, it's the nature center. I thought it was a grand spot."

"Oh, Brogan." Kira walked forward and turned in a circle, studying the area from every angle. To the left, she could see trailhead markers where people could climb higher into the hills. At the front, more trails were marked, and Kira imagined those would be the gentle routes for beginners. It offered everything a person could want – mountain views, ocean views, and trail options as far as the eye could see.

"It's perfect. It's absolutely perfect," Kira crowed.

"I thought so too. It took a while to pick it, but I kept coming back here. It was the least disruptive spot to the environment. Finally, I just went with my gut."

"That's always the best," Kira agreed, walking the length of one side of the rectangle. "Brogan, this is huge. Much bigger than I was expecting."

"I know. I think once we'd decided to add a café and a classroom, I realized I'd need more space. Now, we can have two exhibit rooms, the café, a classroom, and an outdoor seating area. I even designed a little art studio off the classroom. Kids enjoy exploring nature through art, so I thought it might be fun to have some activities for them as well."

"Of course. Brogan, you've thought of everything. I'm so impressed. How will people get here?" Kira turned and studied the surrounding area again.

"That's the kicker – there's a road just past the ledge there." Brogan pointed behind them. "You won't be able to see it from the center, and we'll pave a path from the parking lot so people in wheelchairs can have easy access. But the car traffic won't disturb the peace here."

"Brogan." Kira walked to him and wrapped her arms around his waist. "This is going to be a mad success. I'm so proud of you."

"Thank you. I hope people will like it. I hope Gran is happy with how I'm using the land."

"I'm sure she is. You're building something beautiful here, for generations to enjoy. A legacy, really. Brogan, I think you've planted yourself."

"Have I then?" Brogan laughed down at her.

"You have. Your roots are here now. This is home."

"Aye, it is. It feels good, you know. Really, really good."

"I'm glad for you, I am. Thank you for taking me on this journey with you."

"I'll need your input on the displays, art classes, and so on. But I'm not there yet."

"I'll take all the photographs you need. And my Mam would be more than delighted to lend her art skills to teaching. She loves kids."

"Does she?"

"Of course. She's been bemoaning the lack of grand-children for years now."

"You're hardly past your prime years," Brogan laughed. "You've plenty of time for babies."

"Is that something you want? A family? Children?" That little tidbit of information, Kira realized, might be very important for her future decisions.

"I always thought I didn't. Maybe because I didn't have a particularly happy childhood. And then I just... did. I was sitting outside a pub one day and I saw a happy little toddler and a couple embracing and I thought... I want that. I *really* want that. It was news to me, to be honest."

"But at least you know now. That's something, isn't it?"

"It is. What about you, Kira? Fancy being a mother someday?"

"I've never given it much thought," Kira answered honestly, watching his face carefully. "I can't say it's been a huge desire in my life."

"Do you know why? It sounds like you have a nice relationship with your parents."

"I do. My parents are the best. It's sorry I am that you didn't get to experience the type of upbringing I had. But... I guess I've been so very focused on building my career that I never really considered how children would fit into the mix."

"Do you *like* children?" Brogan wrapped his arm around her shoulders and some of the tension eased. She'd been worried he'd be disappointed in her response.

"I do, yes. I like their lack of restraint. It makes for good photography, because they haven't yet learned to put up walls."

"But you don't see yourself being a mother."

"I don't, no. But it doesn't mean that can't change. I just... I haven't thought much about it. Obviously, lugging a baby along on my shoots wouldn't make much sense. My career has really been my baby. I'm not sure if that makes me sound selfish."

"It doesn't. Nobody would judge a man for those same thoughts."

"I suppose."

"What if you were with a partner who would take some of the burden off you? One willing to watch the baby while you were on shoots?"

Kira laughed. "Does such a man exist?"

"Of course. I'd be willing to do that," Brogan said.

"Oh, Brogan, you're a dear. But can you really say that? You have no idea how much time this nature center will demand of you. If I'm away on a shoot, that would mean you're a full-time daddy while also running a business. It's not that easy."

"I'd have help, I suspect. Judging from how involved everyone is here, I'm sure I'd be able to find someone to care for the baby when I'm busy."

"And that's it, then? You've got it all figured out?" Kira asked, nonplussed.

"I'm just pointing out that there are always solutions to problems," Brogan said pragmatically.

"I don't know how I feel about all of this," Kira said, nerves fluttering in her stomach. Everything in her screamed that she wanted Brogan, but it felt like she was also being expected to change her entire life. It was too much, too soon.

"Luckily, we used condoms so this is not a discussion we have to address anytime soon." Brogan seemed to sense the panic rising in Kira. Turning, he pressed a kiss to her lips. "I've only asked you for time, Kira. I'm not asking you to change your stance on motherhood or to give up a career you love. I was just pointing out that it doesn't have to be all or nothing."

Then why, Kira wondered, did it feel that way?

CHAPTER 25

*T*he weeks passed by in a blur of activity. With the lovely spring weather, more tourists visited the area and Kira was kept hopping at the gallery. True to Morgan's prediction, her prints had sold out almost instantly and she'd been busy creating various-sized versions of them ever since.

"That's another thirty Mr. Murphys sold just this morning on the internet," Morgan called to Kira, who was working the printer in the backroom. It tickled Kira to think about the real Mr. Murphy for sale.

"I really can't believe how much these photos have taken off."

"Mr. Murphy is now our bestseller. He might even be trending." Morgan leaned against the doorjamb to the printer room. "Have you considered hiring help?"

"Me? For what?"

"To take care of these prints. That way, you can be outside taking more photos. Your talents are wasted back here."

"I like framing up my photos," Kira protested.

"Sure and they look lovely. But, Kira… you won't be able to keep up with the demand. We've just had an order for two hundred of your prints for a gift shop in Dublin. How long will that take you to fulfill?"

"Two hundred?" Kira squealed.

"Aye. Of course, we'll negotiate price and offer at cost. Still, that's a nice order, isn't it? Just imagine what else you could be doing with your time. In fact, I may put my foot down and insist on hiring. I've just the person in mind for the job as well."

"But… wait, are you kicking me out?"

"Your talent is wasted here. I've got the girl coming in at noon to train."

"You already hired her?"

"On a trial basis."

"Does my Mam know?"

"Sure and I don't need to be bothering Aislinn on her extended holiday, now do I? I've made great success with our galleries based on my own management decisions."

Kira recognized the light of war in Morgan's pretty eyes.

"All right, all right. I'll back away from the prints."

"Take your camera. Get outside. I want more photos to sell. You're boosting our sales quite nicely."

"Gee, is that all I am to you? A cash cow?"

"Thank the goddess one of us cares about numbers. You and your Mam would give your art away without a second thought."

"That's the truth of it," Kira laughed. "We do have trouble pricing our work."

"Which is why you need me to be handling it for you. Now. Get me some pretty pictures. What about some of the fishing boats? People seem drawn to those types of paintings."

"Fishing boats. Got it. I'll see what I can manage to scrabble together for you."

"Perfect. I'll expect at least three solid images."

"Bossy," Kira muttered as she brushed past.

"Thank you. I take that as a compliment," Morgan called after her.

Kira clattered up the back stairs to her studio apartment. She collected her camera, pausing to study the mussed sheets. Brogan had stayed with her last night, and the memories of being with him flooded her with warmth.

They'd fallen into the habit of spending every night together. They had a standing date night each week with the other two couples, coming together for dinner and drinks at Gallagher's, or sometimes at Liam and Fi's so Liam could try to assert his dominance at darts. Other nights, Kira would drive out to the cottage after a long day at the gallery and spend time with Brogan going over any new developments to the nature center. It was taxing work, this building of a new idea, and yet really fulfilling. Kira was as invested as Brogan was, and neither of them tired of discussing their visions for the future of O'Hallahan's Oasis.

The framework had gone up just this week, much to Kira's delight, and she had kept busy photographing the progress of the build. It was going to be a magnificent building, with two outstretched portions mimicking the wings of a bird. The designer had outdone himself, in Kira's opinion.

She sat on the bed for a moment and ran her hand over the sheets. She was happy, she realized. She could feel her joy wash through her with the memories of last night, along with Brogan's emotions. He loved her. Of that, she was sure. They hadn't said it to each other yet, but Kira could feel it.

Her phone rang, startling her from her musings.

"Hello there, Bryson, how are you?" Kira asked by way of greeting. Her agent was a short-tempered man who was a bulldog in negotiations, but was also known for his fairness and loyalty. He'd stood by her through the years, helping her grow her reputation to a rocketing success.

"I'm well, Kira. I've got an incredible opportunity for you today." Bryson wasn't one for small talk, which Kira appreciated.

"Is that right? Tell me."

"I'm sure you've heard of Tainted Roots? The band?"

Tainted Roots was a famous rock group that had exploded onto the scene with their smash hit, *Never Forever*. It was one of those songs she heard everywhere now, in the backgrounds of commercials, playing in shops, and on the radio. They'd followed up their hit with a studio album that had gone platinum, and they were now one of the hottest-selling bands in the world.

"Of course. I'd have to be living under a rock to not have heard of them."

"I sometimes feel like you are, stuck in that little village."

"Now, now. You know I grew up here."

"Nevertheless. Tainted Roots would like to hire you to cover their tour as well as to do their next album cover. This is huge, Kira. Not only is it an astronomical amount of money, but it would cement your reputation as the photographer to the stars. Say you'll do it."

"Wait... I need more information," Kira said, her heart pounding in her chest.

"It's a six-week tour. It starts next week in Glasgow."

"Is this a European tour only?"

"The first round is. Don't be surprised if more dates get added. I'd budget for at least two months."

Two months, Kira thought. The nature center would be well on the way to being finished by then.

"I'm not hearing your normal squeal of excitement. What am I missing here?"

"I'm just... processing, is all. Two months is a long time to be on the road."

"No longer than any of your other assignments, really."

"I suppose."

"I have to let them know today. Get back to me as soon as you can." In typical fashion, Bryson hung up without saying goodbye.

Kira swallowed, her pulse racing. Tainted Roots was the biggest name in rock and roll right now. It would be insane to pass up such an opportunity. This type of chance came few and far between. It was everything she had ever hoped for.

She had to take the job.

If she didn't, she'd be turning her back on her reputation, on her career, on what she wanted for her future. It was only two months, Kira reminded herself. That was nothing, really.

Her decision made, Kira texted Bryson. Picking up her camera, she headed out, her emotions whirling. Instead of going to the water, Kira found herself wandering into Gallagher's. It was too early for service, but Cait had an open-door policy. Kira found the woman herself lifting bottles behind the bar and making little notes in a notebook.

"Kira, what brings you by so early in the day?"

"Morgan kicked me out."

"Did she now? You two have a fight?"

"Hardly. She said I was wasting my talent by framing prints and ordered me out the door to take more pictures."

"Smart woman. Though if you try to take another photo of me when I'm not looking, I'll punch you."

"Says the woman who has since hung said photo." Kira wandered to where her photographs hung in a funky little trio on the wall next to the bar.

"I was out-voted."

"A good thing too. It's a great photograph," Kira said, studying her work. Listlessly, she turned and began to pace.

"Well, go on then. What's on your mind?"

"Why do you think something's on my mind?"

"I know a mood when I see one. So either I can be reading your mind or you can just tell me straight out. As Aislinn's not around, I'll be acting as your surrogate mother. Is it Brogan then?"

"No. Yes. No."

"That's clear as mud, isn't it? Would you like a little something? Calm your nerves?"

"It's too early. Isn't it?"

"Not for an Irish coffee. I'll join you." Cait wiped her hands on the towel tucked at her waist and began the prep for their coffees. "I like Brogan. And I like you both together. You balance each other nicely."

"He's great," Kira agreed, plopping onto a stool and putting her chin in her hand. Cait's eyes met hers in the mirror above the bar.

"That doesn't sound like ringing praise. You've grown bored of him then?"

"No, not at all."

"Then why the face?" Cait turned and slid a coffee in a glass cup over to her, then bent to pull a metal bowl of heavy cream from the cooler and dashed some on top of the coffee.

"I find myself in a predicament. Well, not really. I've made a choice. But it is not filling me with the joy I had expected it to."

"Tell me." Cait ducked through the passthrough and rounded the bar to heave herself up onto the stool.

"I've been offered the job of a lifetime," Kira said. She took her time explaining to Cait what the job would entail, how it would boost her career and her portfolio, and how long she'd have to be on the road. By the time she'd finished, half their coffees were gone.

"And you've gone and said yes already."

"I did. He needed to know today. The tour starts in Glasgow next week."

"Next week! That's hardly any time to prepare. What about the gallery? What about the nature center?"

"Morgan's hiring help today. Mam's home soon. And they don't need me to finish building the nature center," Kira pointed out gently.

"So that's it then? You just leave it all behind with no concern for people's feelings?"

"It's not like I'm moving across the world, Cait. I'm just taking a job for a few months. Of all people, you have to know how important a career is to a woman."

"Aye, I do know that." Cait sipped her coffee thoughtfully before continuing, "And I'm not disregarding what you've built for yourself. But you've also been building something here, in case you haven't noticed."

"Building what, Cait?" Kira jumped up, too agitated to sit still. "It's not like I've taken any illustrious assignments since I've been here. And don't say the nature center, because – despite my involvement and sincere wish for it to succeed – it's not mine. It's Brogan's. That's his baby, not mine."

"I'm not talking about the nature center, though I do think you're more invested than you realize. I'm talking about *you*. Your future. It's right in front of your eyes but you're too stubborn to see it."

"That's hardly fair, Cait. I am considering my future. That's why I accepted this gig."

"Come here." Cait jumped down and dragged Kira over to the photos she'd hung on the wall. "Just look at these photos. This is art, Kira. Your art. And it matters. These are people and emotions and history... and your love shines through in each one. It's palpable. I'm not saying your photos of rock stars aren't gorgeous –"

"Gee, thanks," Kira muttered.

"– but," Cait continued, tapping the photo of Mr. Murphy, "you show me one photo you've taken of a famous person that has more emotion than this one. I bet you can't. This was taken with love. It shows. And you've made other people feel with this photo. Morgan says it's selling like crazy."

"It is," Kira whispered.

"So?"

"Cait… it's like two different playing fields, though. I could sell hundreds of these prints and never make the money or have the recognition that two months of work with Tainted Roots will give me."

"That's it then? It's about the money, the fame? Is that what really matters to you?"

"It's important for me to be self-sufficient. I insist on making my own money," Kira argued.

"And a proud notion that is, my love. I understand the sentiment. But you're capable of making money in more than one way. How much will be enough for you? You never struck me as someone who needed more and more. I mean, you're living in a tiny studio apartment right now."

"It's not that I need more and more. But it certainly is nice to have money to fall back on. You know I'm not flashy with money, nor do I spend frivolously."

"Then you don't really need the money then, do you? So let's take that out of the picture."

"This gig will be the pinnacle of my career."

"Sure and that's a noble thing to want. I can appreciate the pride you have in your work. But then what?"

"What do you mean?"

"You take this gig and then what? You'll be in high demand, right? Perhaps they'll want you for an American tour. Or the Rolling Stones will call. All well and good, but you'd be on the road more than you think. This gig is more than just a gig. It could change the trajectory of your life."

"But I've been on the road for years. That's certainly not new to me."

"Things have changed." Cait's eyes softened. "Be careful in your choices, Kira. You might not understand what you're giving up."

"Why does it have to be giving something up? Why can't I balance both?"

"Only you can make that decision."

CHAPTER 26

*C*ait's words echoed in Kira's head as she took a tour of the Barrowlands, a Glasgow concert venue, the following week. Tainted Roots had decided to kick off their tour at the iconic venue, as their lead guitar player was from Scotland. Though the venue was small, holding only about two thousand people, it offered a lot of great opportunities for intimate photos of the band interacting with their audience. Kira was looking forward to the show that night, even though her mind was on other things.

Brogan had been beyond understanding when she'd told him about the gig. In fact, he'd been thrilled for her – which, in a weird way, had made her choice even harder. Not once did he ask her to stay, though he'd been honest with her about the fact that he would miss her.

They'd yet to exchange the big L-word, Kira mused as she walked around backstage, checking angles and her sightlines. In fact, they'd yet to discuss whether they were even in a committed relationship. She supposed some things didn't need to be said, for she knew that as long as Brogan was with her, he wouldn't be with anyone else. Nor would she, for that matter. Cheating wasn't in her blood. Kira didn't get the excitement of it all, when at the end of the day, those actions were hurting others.

"There's a sight for sore eyes."

Kira turned at the voice. She took a deep breath as Jax approached, doing a quick inventory of her emotions to see how she felt about him. When she realized that she no longer resented him, Kira returned his hug.

"How've you been, Jax?" Kira studied him. He didn't look great, if she was being honest with herself, but maybe most people wouldn't notice what her careful photographer's eye did. Dark shadows rimmed his grey eyes, and he'd lost weight, making his face more angular. He wore his typical get-up – leather pants and a ripped t-shirt – and she could see he'd added more tattoos to his collection.

"Busy, love. Busy, busy, busy. But we're good. Back in the studio when we're not touring. So we'll have a break with this tour."

"Are you on tour with Tainted Roots?" Kira asked, surprised that Bryson had failed to mention *that* particular tidbit of information. She imagined he'd known she'd be likely to refuse if he'd told her. Making a mental note to call him on it, Kira focused back on Jax.

"Aye, love. I'm the one who told Tainted Roots to look you up. They loved our album cover. Told them they have to go with the best."

"I appreciate that, Jax." Despite his self-centeredness, the man did have some redeeming qualities. "You look tired."

"You know how it is. Late nights on tour. Always on to the next city. I can sleep when I'm dead, love."

"Don't wear yourself out." Kira patted his arm. "Your fans would be devastated."

"Jax, let's go over the setlist," a voice called from the back.

"See ya after? We're going out. Say you'll join? Like old times?" Jax winked at her.

"Not like old times, Jax. I have someone now."

"Ah, well. Lucky bastard. Still, you'll join us?"

"I'll see you after the show. Knock 'em dead tonight."

"I always do, love. I always do." Jax trotted away.

Kira felt a wry sort of fondness for the man, like one would for an incorrigible puppy, but no longer did he have a hold on her heart. She'd have to let Brogan know that Jax was on tour, though, as she wouldn't want him to think she had withheld information from him. Kira picked up her phone to text him, but was interrupted by the manager.

"Let's go over the shots I'd like to see for tonight."

"Right, of course," Kira said. "I'm particularly fond of this angle. Look, see how the lights shine down, but I'll still be able to capture the audience…"

A very sweaty eight hours later, Kira found herself pressed into a booth at a local club with a mix of groupies, band members, and stage crew. She hadn't had time to shower or change; she'd been swept up in the backstage crowd calling to her after the show.

The concert had been… outstanding, really. She could see why Tainted Roots had made a name for themselves. The intimacy of the small venue had led to much more audience interaction, and if the concertgoers hadn't been in love with the band before the show, they certainly were after. Kira was certain she'd gotten some of her best shots of the night when the lead singer had jumped into the crowd and slung an arm over a fan's shoulders, still singing into the microphone.

Now the energy still buzzed, everyone riding the high from an awesome show, and the drinks flowed like water.

"Whiskey?" Jax plopped down next to her with a bottle.

"I've got one already." Kira pointed to her largely untouched glass.

"Did you enjoy the show?"

"You were great, Jax," Kira said dutifully.

"Someday, we'll have bands like Tainted Roots opening for us," Jax promised.

"I don't doubt it. Your talent was never something I questioned."

Jax winked at her. "Just my lovemaking then?"

"You didn't love me."

"I love every woman when I'm with her."

"You're shameless." Kira laughed.

"Ach, I'm a realist. The road's no place for a relationship, love. I've resigned myself to that fact."

"Have you? I thought you quite enjoyed sampling the menu." Kira teased and then blinked as a bright flash blinded her for a moment.

"No pictures!" Jax glared and the photographer slinked away. Turning back to Kira, he shrugged. "I'm not meant to be tied down. At least not at this point in my life. That's for later."

"What happens if you meet someone on the way?

Someone who derails you?" Kira wasn't sure if she was asking him or herself.

"Is this your man we're talking about then?" Unusually perceptive, Jax squinted at her as he rolled a cigarette.

"It was a general question, but yes, I suppose."

"I think if someone hits me hard enough to derail me, then I'd have to figure out how to get back on track with them at my side. A passenger on my train, I suppose."

"But what if they don't want to ride on your train? What if they wanted a quieter life?"

"It would be tough to figure out. But if it was worth it? Yeah, I'd do it. But right now? Nobody I've met has been worth giving up my dream. That's what keeps me warm at night."

"And a plethora of willing women," Kira pointed out.

"That too, love. Speaking of which…" Jax leered at a groupie across the club. "I've an eye on one now."

"Wear condoms," Kira instructed.

"Always do."

Kira sipped her whiskey and thought about what he'd said. The music of the club drifted around her, as did people's voices. It was a busy, loud, and hectic place, this club filled with people trying to out-famous each other, and she craved the stillness of nature instead.

She didn't want to be here.

Kira put her whiskey down in confusion as the absolute certainty that she'd made the wrong decision flooded her. This scene… these people? They were no longer her people. She didn't want this for her life.

She wanted to watch baby otters paddle about in a pond overlooking a field of wildflowers. She wanted to watch the nature center get built up, and to take photos that showcased the beauty of what Ireland had to offer.

Just because she *could* be here didn't mean she should be. This was wrong, Kira realized now, wrong for what she wanted out of life. She'd been so certain that this gig would be the highlight of her career but now all she wanted was to be tucked back in a tiny gallery framing her prints and seeing people's joy when they purchased something she'd created.

That was what she'd been missing, she realized. That human connection. Because her work was displayed on such a large scale, she never got to see a person holding up an album cover and marveling over her work. But time after time in the gallery, she'd heard people exclaim in excitement over the images she'd created.

"Want to do a line?" A roadie squeezed in next to her and leaned over, his breath noxious with cigarette smoke, and displayed a little bottle of white powder.

"No, thank you. In fact, I have to be going."

"Where ya going, love? It's barely three in the morning." The man laughed as Kira squeezed past him and out of the busy club. Grateful for the cool air that greeted her outside, Kira gulped it in and wondered how Bryson was going to take her decision.

Not well, she suspected, but that was his problem to deal with.

Kira knew it was too late to call Brogan when she got back to her hotel room. Instead, she indulged in a hot bath to soak her sore feet and clambered naked under the crisp white hotel sheets. Dropping into a dreamless sleep, Kira blinked awake at her alarm only a few short hours later.

"I forgot how annoying this was," she muttered. Late nights and early travel times were the usual for touring, and it was not an aspect of being on the road that Kira enjoyed. Desperately needing coffee, she sat up and grabbed her phone as it buzzed with a call.

"Gracie!"

"What the hell, Kira?"

"Excuse me?" Kira blinked.

"I love you and all, but there's just no excuse for this."

"I'll need you to elaborate. I haven't had my coffee."

"Have a late night, did ye?"

"Of course. I was photographing a rock concert."

"You didn't tell me you'd be with Jax again."

"I didn't know." Kira closed her eyes and took a deep breath. "It was good, though, Gracie. It was really nice to see him."

"And so that's it? You're tossing Brogan to the side for a self-centered rock star?"

"What? No, I meant because I realized I no longer resent him. He's just not for me."

"Well, the photos suggest otherwise."

"What photos?"

"Open your text messages. I sent you about a billion because you didn't answer my calls."

"I didn't hear the phone. I was dead to the world. Hold on." Kira scrolled to message apps and saw she had a ton of new messages. None from Brogan though. "Oh no."

At the head of some gossip blog or another, the headline ran: *Has Jax reunited with his former flame?* The photo beneath it was the one where Jax was leering at her and she was laughing at him. To an outside observer, it would look like Kira was besotted with Jax.

"Has Brogan seen this?"

"I don't know. I can't get a hold of him."

"I'm coming home, Gracie. I already decided last night. This isn't what I want anymore."

"You'd better get here fast, before you lose everything you've worked toward. And I don't mean your career." With that, Gracie clicked off, leaving Kira blinking at her phone in panic.

When Brogan's phone went right to voicemail, Kira booked a flight.

he short flight from Glasgow to Dublin was torture. From Dublin, Kira had opted to continue on the flight over to Shannon instead of driving across the country. At each stop, she'd tried phoning Brogan, but he never once picked up.

Why had she gone to the club after the concert?

Repeatedly, Kira alternated between berating herself and reminding herself that she hadn't actually done anything wrong. Why hadn't she sent Brogan the text about Jax when she'd meant to? If she had, she could have avoided this whole mess. Now, she was convinced Brogan was freezing her out. As he had a right to, she thought. Kira was the one who had up and left him.

She thought about all the times he'd been betrayed by his mother. Despite the shields she'd put up, Kira had been privy to a lot more memories than maybe Brogan had realized or wanted her to know. They had painted an unhappy picture of a boy who was consistently rejected by his own mother. No matter how many times Brogan had tried to reach out, even when he was older, she'd refused to work on their problems, admit she was wrong, or engage in any behavior that wasn't self-serving.

But still, he'd tried.

That was the kind of man Brogan was, she realized. He didn't give up on people; he kept trying to see the good. It was a miracle that he'd become the person he had after an upbringing such as his. Kira's worry was that he would be less tolerant with her. Brogan had every right to move on from her if he chose to – not only because of the Jax situation, but because she had chosen her career over him.

He hadn't seen it like that at the time. He'd been excited for her. But how much was a man supposed to take? Kira worried that the Jax photo would push Brogan into giving up on her.

It was mid-afternoon by the time she reached the small village of Grace's Cove, speeding as fast as she could in her little rental car. Kira didn't even stop in town, but blew past the village and headed toward Brogan's cottage. She'd called Gracie from the airport with explicit instructions to call her if she heard any word of Brogan's location. Her phone hadn't rung, so Kira decided to start with his cottage. Damn the man for ignoring her calls! One way or the other, they were going to have this out.

Her pulse raced as she drummed her fingers on the steering wheel. Bryson had screamed at her over the phone this morning when she'd terminated the contract. Not only would he lose money on the deal, but also credibility. She apologized profusely, but he hadn't been in the place to hear it, and he'd fired her on the spot. So much for long-time loyalty, Kira thought. Hoping he would calm down and understand where she was coming from, Kira had carried on with her plan. Leaving the hotel this morning and waving to the people boarding the tour bus had felt a little like racing away from school when it was let out for summer holidays.

For the first time in ages, Kira felt free.

Which was weird, she knew, because her whole career had been built around the freedom of making her own choices. But there was something different this time, something much larger. Kira wasn't just leaving a gig – she was changing her life.

Having that choice, and using it, was where true freedom lived.

Kira let out a little woosh of air when she saw that Brogan's car was at his cottage. Hopping out, she ran to the door and knocked repeatedly. When nobody answered, Kira tried the handle. Not caring if she was breaking and entering, Kira popped inside and raced around the cottage, only to find it empty. Damn it! Where was the man?

Running back outside, she stood, torn as to which trail-head to take.

"Where is he?" Kira asked, lifting her face to the clouds above.

"He's at the pond."

Kira turned to see the faint outline of Fiona hovering outside the cottage. "Fiona!"

"I'm glad you're back. It was stupid of you to go."

"Lovely. Can we have this chat another time?" Kira turned to head for the pond.

"Do you love him?"

"What?" Kira turned back to look at Fiona.

"You heard me, girl."

"I…"

"If you don't love him, then get back in the car and go home." Fiona's voice was harsh, immediately causing Kira to hunch her shoulders.

"Why would you say that?"

"Because he deserves someone to put him first. He puts everyone and everything else first. Including nature."

"That's why I'm here. I left my job. I'm here for him."

"You still didn't answer my question. Do you love him?"

"Aye, I do," Kira whispered, feeling the truth of it race through her all the way to her toes.

"Then tell him that. Don't make him be the first to say it."

"I won't. I promise. I'm going to him now."

But Fiona was already gone.

Kira raced down the trail to the pond, slipping and sliding in her flat-soled shoes, wishing she'd thought this through a little more. Gasping, she arrived at the pond to see Brogan crouched by the water, his back to her.

"Brogan!"

Brogan started and almost fell backward onto his butt. He turned and a wide smile broke his face. He hopped up, racing across the pond toward her.

"Kira! What are you doing here?" Brogan caught her in a big hug, his arms feeling like home to her, and lifted her in a swirling circle.

"I had to see you," Kira said against his mouth.

"Well, I've missed you, too." Brogan could barely get the words in, she was kissing him so hard. Finally, Kira broke the kiss and pressed her hands to his face, her breath coming heavy in her chest. "Is everything okay?"

"Brogan, I love you. I should've said it sooner. I love you so much. I'm sorry for leaving you. I shouldn't have left you like that."

Happiness flushed Brogan's face, his eyes lighting up, though a touch of sadness lingered there. Kira wanted to make love to him until the sadness drained away from him forever.

"I love you too, Kira. I have for a long time now. But I wanted to give you time."

"I should have told you. Before I left. And I shouldn't have left."

"Kira, it's okay. It was a huge job for you. I was excited for you to have this opportunity."

"But it's not what I want anymore. Maybe I needed to go and experience it to realize I didn't."

"What do you want then?" Brogan grabbed her hand and tugged her with him to walk around the edge of the pond.

"I want to be here. With you. I want to create art for the people – images that anyone can buy and hang in their home. Work that will bring a smile to someone's heart."

"You can do that here."

"I can. I have. I didn't realize how much I would enjoy it. It's not losing my career, it's just shifting the focus."

"You're brilliant, Kira. Anything you focus on will be a success, I'm sure of it."

"Brogan… I have to show you something." Kira stopped him and turned him to her. "And I need to tell you how sorry I am. I didn't know he'd be on the tour, and I meant to tell you as soon as I found out but the stage manager interrupted me and then I was on duty and –"

Brogan just looked down at her patiently.

"Jax's band was opening for Tainted Roots. I spoke with him last night at the club after the show. Well, someone took a picture and then the blogs implied we were back together." Kira pulled her phone from her pocket with the intention to show him.

"I know. I saw."

"Wait… what? You saw the photo?"

"Of course. A few people sent it to me."

"And… you're not mad at me?"

"Did you do anything I should be mad about?" Brogan regarded her, his eyes clear.

"No, of course not. I would *never*. In fact, it was kind of nice seeing him, because I realized that I don't resent him anymore. He's sort of like a dopey puppy you tolerate."

"I told you I trusted you, did I not? And how important honesty was to me?"

"You have, yes."

"You've given me no reason not to believe your word, Kira. I didn't think for a minute you were out hooking up with Jax last night."

"Really? I was so worried that this photo would hurt you." Tears sprang to Kira's eyes, and Brogan reached out and brushed one away with his finger. "I would hate for you to feel like you weren't important to me."

"I know I can trust you, Kira. And I hope you know you can trust me. There are going to be times when we travel or are apart. I don't want to think twice or worry about what the other person is doing. I wouldn't be able to be in a relationship with you if I thought you were capable of doing something like that."

"Oh, Brogan, you really are the best thing that's ever happened to me." Kira collapsed against him, wrapping her arms around his waist and pressing her ear to his chest. The tension of the day eased from her shoulders as his arms came around her.

"Now, I have a surprise for you."

"You do? Brogan, why didn't you answer your phone then? I've been calling you all day. I was convinced you were avoiding me."

"Ach, that silly phone. I forgot it at the cottage." Brogan shrugged, looking sheepish. "Come on. Look."

"You have the new fortress up!" Kira exclaimed.

"I do. But that's not what I want you to look at. Look behind it. On land, in the brush under the wood."

Kira crouched next to Brogan and peered inside.

"She had her babies!"

"Two of them. That's where I was all day. I didn't want to bother her, but I wanted to make sure everything was going along smoothly and all."

Friends. I'm a father.

Fergal popped his head out of the den and looked up at them.

"A fine father you make, Fergal. How is Heather?"

All is well. A boy and a girl.

"Congratulations then. We'll keep checking on you. If you need anything…"

Fish.

"Of course – fresh fish on the way for you tomorrow, I

promise." Kira turned and squeezed Brogan's arm. "It's a boy and a girl. Everyone's good. Fergal's a proud papa."

"Excellent news. I say this calls for a celebration. May I invite you back to my cottage and have my way with you?"

"I'd love nothing more. I didn't even bring my camera with me," Kira said with a laugh as they began hiking back up toward the cottage. "I was hurrying so fast, I left it in the car. I never do that."

"You were really worried, weren't you?"

"You've changed my life, Brogan. I didn't see how it would work at first, but now it all makes perfect sense. You're the one I've been waiting for."

"I'm glad to hear you saying that, because I was really hoping this wasn't a waste of money," Brogan said, tugging her around the side of the cottage and back toward the garden shed.

Which was no longer a shed, Kira realized. Somehow she'd missed the addition that had been built on the back of it. When had he had time to do this?

Brogan fished a key out and unlocked the door.

Her heart did a funny little dance in her chest when she stepped through to a little photography studio. Brogan had nailed it. It was done in white, with a large glass wall that ran the side of the room. In the area that used to be the garden shed, shelves and cubbies had been installed to house her equipment, and Kira even saw several rolls of backdrops for her to use as backgrounds for her images if she was doing portraits.

"I figured this could be a space for you to work, take photos, do editing... that kind of thing. I'm not sure if I have everything you need here, but I'll work on finding it. I was hoping... well..." Brogan shrugged and let out a little laugh. "That if I made a spot just for you, you'd start to see this as home."

"Brogan... this is home," Kira said, but she wasn't looking at the studio. Instead, she faced him and met his eyes. Leaning forward, she pressed a hand to his heart. "With you, I'm home."

*K*ira blinked back the tears that she couldn't seem to hold inside, even though today was meant to be a happy day. All of her favorite people were gathered together, and music played happily in the background. The sun shone brightly in the sky – a perfect summer day.

"Kira, would you join me for the honors?" Brogan called.

He stood in front of a large ribbon, tied neatly in a bow, which had been strung across the double doors leading into the nature center. The build had finished a month ago, and the interior finishes had been completed just this week.

Dylan, being a smart businessman, had snatched up the housing development's crew and offered double their wages to get the center built by summer. They'd proven to be an excellent and reliable crew of workers. The man who'd attacked the otters had been getting treatment for his mental health, and was serving community service as well, because Brogan had requested leniency.

"Brogan, you should really do this." Kira looked up at him.

"It's as much yours as mine."

"Together, then," Kira insisted.

Brogan put his hands on the scissors with her, and together they cut the ribbon to the cheers of the crowd.

"Welcome, everyone! We hope you rediscover your love for nature here," Brogan called with a smile.

Soon they were swallowed by the crowd of people who moved past them to study the exhibits. The café had prepared a buffet-style layout for food, and the picnic tables set up outside were full of villagers enjoying the view of the ocean.

"I'm so proud of you. We both are." Aislinn and Baird had come to stand by Kira's side, putting their arms around her. "Your prints are beautiful here, darling. I had no idea you could do such good work with a macro lens either."

"Neither did I," Kira laughed. She'd discovered a new passion in her photography, which was not something she'd expected at this point in her career. But when Brogan had broached the subject of taking photos of insects, Kira had gone all in on learning about macro photography. Who knew that so many of the smallest things held such beauty? She'd been delighted to learn that there were still things that could excite her.

"Everyone, I have an announcement to make!" Cait, the de facto mayor of Grace's Cove, tapped her glass and everyone quieted. "A few of you have been asking about who won the bet."

"What bet?" Kira asked.

"Why, the bet on when you'd decide to be with Brogan, of course," Cait said.

"Wait, you bet on us?"

"She's impossible," Fi sighed. "Just deal with it. She bet on her own daughter, if you can believe it."

"As it was a tricky one, what with Kira leaving town to carouse with rock stars and all –"

"I wasn't carousing!"

"– we've decided that the day she came home marks the day they officially got together. Which means the winner is…"

Everyone turned to look at Mr. Murphy, who sat at a table by the café.

"Aislinn!"

"*Mam?*" Kira shouted, turning and glaring at her mother. "You bet on my love life?"

"I bet to win. For the both of us, love."

"I can't believe…" Kira trailed off as Aislinn went to collect her prize.

"Who cares about the bet? I won the best prize of all," Brogan declared. He swooped her into a kiss, then swirled her into a dance.

"You'd better donate that money to the nature center!" Kira shouted over her shoulder, and then fell into the dance, forgetting everything but Brogan's arms around her.

It seemed she'd found her way after all.

AFTERWORD

It's been a difficult year for most people, to say the least. I don't think many of us had expected to ride out a pandemic in our lifetimes, but here we are. I have to say, while there have been times where the darkness of it all can become all-consuming (the arguing on social media, the incredible loss of life, the frustration with lockdowns), I've also been incredibly lifted up by those who are sharing their light during this difficult time. To all the healthcare workers, scientists, teachers, and everyone else who has put everything on the line to try to keep this boat afloat, I give you my sincerest thanks. I, myself, have found that diving into my writing has provided me with my own little escape from the darkness. My hope is that my books will bring you that same light and just for a moment they can offer you escape and hope for brighter days ahead. Sparkle on, my friends!

- Tricia O'Malley (March 2021)

MS. BITCH - CHAPTER 1
FINDING HAPPINESS IS THE BEST REVENGE

About Ms. Bitch:

Inspired by my true story, this book will take you on an adventure that leaves you realizing that you are only one choice away from a different future. Ms. Bitch explores one woman's journey of accepting herself and breaking free of the toxic bonds that hold us back from the life we are truly meant to live.

Here is a sneak peek...

"You quit your job?" Tess pushed back from her desk to see her husband, Gabe, beaming at her as though he'd just won the lottery.

"I did! You know I've been wanting to for a while now, babe." Gabe wrapped his arms around Tess, swinging her into a bouncy two-step.

"Um, not really, no. In the abstract, yes, for when we talked about moving to Colorado, but not like, you know, *now.*" Tess's mind whirled as quickly as Gabe was moving her across the room. Their rescue bulldogs, Red and Ringo, joined in the dance at their feet.

"It just seemed like a good time," Gabe said. "Your books are doing so well, and I have a nice 401k. I think we'll be fine."

"But… why now? Wouldn't it have been better for you to leave once we actually decided to move? I mean, we haven't even explored any of the areas we think we might like to live, yet. What if we decide to stay here?" Tess asked, trying to slow Gabe down without dampening his exuberance.

She hadn't seen him this bubbly in a while – manic

almost – and was trying to enjoy his mood while tamping down on the panic that threatened to choke her. Being thrust into the sole breadwinner position with zero discussion was not something she'd put on her agenda to contemplate this afternoon. Gabe danced her back over to her desk, leaning her back against it to kiss her deeply, and then peeked over her shoulder at her computer.

"Is that for our trip to New Orleans? You should definitely book those concert tickets. Now, we can go and be carefree and relax." Gabe nuzzled into her neck as he held her close.

Tess breathed in his familiar scent, letting him hold her there, and tried to relax into the moment. He'd been stressing over accounts at work, and putting in extra hours at the gym to deal with it for months now. When she'd tried to talk to him about it, he'd nearly bitten her head off more than a time or two. Maybe he did need this change— for both their sakes. At least he might be in a better mood for their trip next week to New Orleans. They'd planned it to celebrate their fifth anniversary, and she'd hoped it would bring him out of his funk and reconnect them.

Tess began calculating how much money they had in their bank accounts, and what would need to be set aside as a safety net now that they couldn't count on Gabe's salary.

"Okay, babe, I'll book the concert tickets. It'll be great. We could use some fun," Tess said, and watched as Gabe bounced away, pausing to tussle with the delighted dogs, before whistling his way downstairs.

The telltale clink of ice cubes hitting a glass and the squeak of the door on the liquor cabinet told Tess just how

Gabe planned to celebrate. Turning, she stared out the window where they'd just had a brand-new cedar fence installed around their beautiful yard, a cost that she'd been willing to spend to keep her dogs safe. It had been her one condition about buying this house with Gabe, and though taking out a home equity loan had bothered her, she'd gone along with it to renovate the house.

Despite herself, she'd gotten caught up in the fun of it and they'd overhauled the kitchen, added a deck to the backyard, and made improvements to Gabe's man-room in the basement. All while they'd still talked about moving to Colorado. Tess shook her head and wondered at their decision-making, but a part of her never really thought they'd make the move out of Illinois. It had been somewhat of a pipe dream for so long, one of those 'what-ifs' they always talked about. She'd been shocked when Gabe had agreed to book a trip to Colorado that spring to explore neighborhoods. Now, she contemplated what her life would be like with Gabe at home every day, and her nails dug into her palms. She loved her husband, but she also loved being able to focus on her work at home uninterrupted.

"Tess, come have a drink with me," Gabe called up the stairs, and Tess glanced back to where she'd planned to work on a chapter for her next novel. "We should celebrate – this is the start of a new life for us."

A week later, Tess stood beside Gabe in the sparkling marble foyer of their favorite hotel in New Orleans, admiring the graceful arches and high ceilings that added to the old-world charm.

"Welcome back, Mr. and Mrs. Campbell." The woman at the front desk beamed at them, sliding keys across the gleaming wood counter to Gabe. "And, may I say? Happy anniversary."

"Thank you," Tess said, smiling at the woman before following Gabe to the elevator. She loved coming here. There was nothing like escaping to another place, and the pulse of this city never ceased to excite her. Not to mention the location of the hotel was fantastic.

"Ta-da," Gabe proclaimed, coming to stop at the end of a long hallway, carpeted with the traditional fleur-de-lis pattern. He held his hands up to the door with a gilded sign proclaiming it to be the Tennessee Williams suite.

"Gabe! Did you upgrade us? I didn't reserve us a suite." Delighted at his forethought, she pulled out her phone to take a picture of the door. "Tennessee Williams! My readers are going to love this!"

"No," Gabe said, his tone sharp as he grabbed the phone from her hands. "I don't want you posting anything publicly about this trip."

"What… why? It's just a suite name. It's a famous author, I'm sure my readers would like it."

"I said no. You know I don't like it when you post about me on your author page. This trip is private. That's non-negotiable." Gabe pushed the door open to reveal a large suite, with floor-to-ceiling windows, a wrap-around balcony, and a huge seating area with a green velvet sofa and a bookcase packed with vintage books. "I want this to be just between us, Tess. This is our time."

Tess wanted to protest that she rarely posted anything about Gabe publicly, but he was already drawing her into the suite. She let the moment go to exclaim over the room as he threw the balcony doors open, letting in the full cacophony of New Orleans, and Tess joined him to look down at the people meandering the street below.

"Oh, look! A second-line." Tess smiled down at where a bride in a vintage-style gown and a groom with bright blue shoes paraded their way down the street behind a brass band.

The first time they'd visited New Orleans together, they'd jumped up from their meal and had run outside to see the parade dance by. Not only had it been exciting, but that moment turned out to be what inspired them to return to the French Quarter to get married. "Remember ours? It was so much fun!" She leaned into him, wishing he'd put his arm around her.

"Right? Time for drinks." Gabe barely glanced at the couple who pirouetted below them, lost in their bliss. Tess wondered if she'd looked that happy on their wedding day. She'd been so nervous that the day had flown by in a flash.

Reluctantly, she followed Gabe inside where he handed her a drink from the mini bar – the first of many they'd have that weekend. In New Orleans, cocktails were abundant.

The following day, they poked around the French Quarter, popping into antique jewelry shops until Gabe could find a necklace he liked for her as a memento of their anniversary. It was her credit card that paid for it, but Tess pushed the annoyance away, reminding herself that finances blend together after marriage. The biggest surprise came that evening when Gabe presented her with a private dinner on the balcony of their suite, complete with flowers and even more gifts – diamonds this time. Tess wanted to enjoy the romance, but she couldn't help desperately wondering who the person sitting across from her was. It was like watching someone tick off all the boxes on the checklist: flowers? Check. Diamonds? Check. Fancy surprise dinner on a private balcony? Check. Yet he hadn't touched her since they'd arrived.

Pasting a smile on her face, Tess chattered her way through dinner, and kept the conversation going on the walk to the Preservation Hall's famous jazz concert. As they stood in line to wait, a woman in front of them turned and glanced at Tess's sparkly dress, something she'd bought special for the occasion, hoping Gabe would think she looked sexy for their anniversary.

"Smashing dress, darling," the woman said, and Tess smiled her thanks before quickly glancing at Gabe to see if he would think the same. Instead, he downed the drink he'd brought on the walk with them and tossed the cup in a nearby garbage container. Ignoring her misgivings, Tess found their seats, and for the next hour, had the first moments of pure joy on this trip since they'd arrived. They sat on an unforgiving wooden school bench, a few feet from an old-timey jazz band, and listened as the band poured their souls into their music. Tess was delighted.

"What a great band! I'm so glad we went this time," Tess exclaimed after the concert while she waited at the bar for Gabe to order drinks for the walk home. She didn't even want a drink – she was riding high on the excitement of the show – but took the one he handed her nonetheless.

"They had such a funky vibe," Gabe agreed, as they wound their way back to the hotel. "I love how they all dressed the part too. It'd be cool to sit in a pub and hear their stories."

"Totally." Tess was already dreaming up characters around the musicians. "Their faces had so much personality, too. But the music… it really just kind of hit you in your soul."

Gabe let them into the suite and strode into the bedroom where he stripped and wrapped himself in a robe, before moving to the mini-fridge where he'd stored a bottle. Tess put her still-full drink on the table, and dug in her luggage before stepping to the bathroom.

"I'll just be a minute."

In the bathroom, Tess examined her hair and make-up as she slithered into a little red teddy she'd bought just for tonight, hoping that some hot anniversary sex would bring them closer again. Lately, she'd felt like the supporting role in Gabe's life, but never the leading.

"Hey," Tess said, standing in the doorway and posing for him. Gabe lay on the bed, wrapped in his robe, scrolling his phone.

"Oh, hey," Gabe said, and the look that crossed his face wasn't a particularly happy one – more like a grimace, if Tess was honest with herself. She knew what he was going to say before the words even came out of his mouth. "Babe, I can't tonight. I ate way too much food at dinner. Can we just chill instead?"

"Of course," Tess said lightly, so as not to cause a fight. She reached behind her to pull the fluffy white robe from the door. "I'm just going to sit on the balcony for a bit then."

"Sure." Gabe didn't look up as he typed on his phone. Tess picked up her Kindle and unhinged the swinging balcony door to sit where they'd had dinner earlier that evening. The melody of the city embraced her, and Tess glanced back over her shoulder, hoping Gabe would join her. Instead, she could just see his face, alight in the glow of his phone, a smug smile across his handsome features as he continued to type rapidly, a bottle of whiskey on the side table.

Tess blinked back tears as she turned away, burying herself in her book, forcing the questions down for another day.

He looked so happy in the photo. Tess sat, staring numbly at the computer screen in front of her where Gabe's Face-book Messenger sat wide open, the picture of her husband – naked in bed, his arms wrapped around a woman too young to know the difference between lust and love – searing into her retinas. Tess knew that look on his face – she'd seen it time and again after he'd satisfied himself with her body – a smile playing on his lips while she waited for him to come back from the bathroom with a tissue, stuck in the universally awkward situation that lovers often find themselves in.

Tess's hands trembled as she opened another browser window and slowly typed in the web address of their bank. The accounts popped onto the screen – at least the accounts they shared – and the tightness that had banded her chest eased a bit as she saw that all looked to be normal. The money in the shared account was mainly hers, as it had now been several months since Gabe had quit his job and embarked on a steady regimen of going to the gym twice a day and drinking too much.

Tess hesitated, her eyes flashing back to the picture on the screen in front of her, taking in the smug satisfaction on Gabe's handsome face, before calmly emptying their shared bank account and moving all the money to hers. She waited, taking one shuddering breath after another, to see if something would happen – anything – but only a blast of wind at the window and a silent house answered. What did she think would happen? Her phone would explode with angry texts or sirens would go off? It wasn't like she was doing anything illegal. Or immoral.

Her mind flashed to just days before, when she'd lain awake, watching the light from Gabe's phone blink, flashing repeatedly across the ceiling, incessantly pounding its message into Tess's brain. Gabe slept on, not a care in the world, while the blinking light refused to be ignored, his phone all but screaming at Tess.

Wake up, you fucking moron.

She'd slid from the covers, the air cool on her clammy skin, and padded around the bed. Tess had hesitated as she stood over Gabe, watching him sleep so peacefully, and wondered again if she was being paranoid. Perhaps she'd been imagining his distance from her lately. Her hand had hovered over the phone for a moment before she'd made up her mind and snatched it from the table. Racing around the bed, Tess had caught her toe on a nightstand as she headed for the bathroom, and unable to control the curse that shot from her mouth, she'd hobbled her way to the bathroom door.

But not in time.

Gabe had been on her in seconds, slamming her into the tiled wall of the bathroom as carelessly as if she were one of his sagging intramural football buddies, wrenching the phone from her hand before she'd had time to recover from the pain that still ratcheted up her leg from her stubbed toe. The crack of her head against the cold tile of the wall echoed the crack in her heart and she watched, astounded, as tears filled Gabe's eyes. He was crying?

"Oh, baby. Stop this. You know I don't want you on my phone. We've promised to trust each other. Don't do this."

He'd gone back to bed then, never asking her if she was okay, his phone tucked beneath his pillow. Asleep in moments, Gabe had acted like nothing had happened the next day.

Now Tess stared at the computer screen, her brain working in overdrive as she tried to process all the ways their lives were intertwined. Opening another browser, she systematically began to change the passwords to all her business accounts, a little zing of power zipping through her at each change she made. *Her* business email accounts. Zing! *Her* business vendors. Zing! *Her* business shared folders. Zing! *Her* mobile accounts. At that one, Tess paused. Curious, she clicked on Gabe's phone statement. It didn't take long to figure out the number that had been lighting up his line for so many months. Methodically, Tess screenshotted the number, as icily detached as she could be. Gathering information.

Building her walls.

She'd asked him, hadn't she? Repeatedly. Was something wrong? Was there something he'd wanted to tell her?

She'd even asked him to his face – is there someone else? Gabe had assured her that he was just dealing with the stress of leaving his job – something that Tess had done everything in her power not to remind him he'd brought upon himself – and had brushed off her worried questions. She'd let it drop, knowing men tended to clam up when stressed.

Now she scanned the phone records, looking back for months as the text messages continued to that same number. Thousands of Facebook messages streamed before her, months of infidelity laid out in vivid, graphic detail, her future crumbling around her. Tess copied it all, saving the file to her password-protected shared drive. She nosed through any other important documentation she could find on Gabe's computer until there was nothing else to be found – nothing else she could do except confront her husband.

Tess sat still, frozen as the end of her marriage loomed. She waited in silence when the front door opened. She waited as Gabe greeted the dogs. She listened as he whistled down the hallway – cheerful, she imagined, from his most recent orgasm – until he rounded the corner into his office.

"Why are you on my computer?" Gabe's face contorted in rage.

Tess's hands clenched, and she shifted the chair, turning enough so he could see the picture on the screen behind her.

"It's over."

"Tess, that's not what you think," Gabe said, stepping

forward to put his hands out, but dropping them at her look.

"I knew it. I *knew* it! I should've trusted my gut, but I let your voice drown out my own. It's over, Gabe. There's no way I – no, *we* – can come back from this," Tess said, her voice cold as betrayal sliced through her.

"Okay, let's just talk about this rationally. That woman means nothing," Gabe insisted, pacing in front of his desk, the dogs following his movement.

"Nothing? Really?" Tess turned to read some of the messages. "'I love you, Babers' — ick, *babers*? — 'I can't wait to have you in my arms again. We're meant to be together.' Really, Gabe?"

"That's just bullshit. You shouldn't be reading that crap. It means nothing," Gabe slammed his hand on the desk, causing the dogs to jump up and pace between them.

"Gag me, you're sending her Disney kissing emojis. What is this girl, fourteen?" Tess bit out, her heart pumping in her chest, sweat trickling at the back of her collar.

"She's in college, and I don't love her. It's not what you think."

She barked out a laugh, turning to look at the naked picture of them in bed together.

"I'm fairly certain I'm quite clear on what this is," Tess said, and raised an eyebrow at him. "A co-worker of yours, I see. I suppose this explains why you left work. Oh... were you fired? I bet you were fired." Tess slammed her own hand down on the desk. "That makes so much sense to me now."

"I was not fired." Gabe's face darkened, anger reaching his voice for the first time. "I chose to leave."

"I bet you were asked to leave, weren't you? For screwing your subordinate. Even for you – what a dipshit move," Tess said. She was so completely fed up with Gabe's lies.

"I said I wasn't fired," Gabe shouted.

Tess laughed at him, knowing it would antagonize him and not even caring.

"Oddly enough, Gabe? I'm having an incredibly hard time believing anything you tell me right now. I can't imagine why." Tess turned back to scan the messages on the computer screen.

"Stop reading those." Gabe tried to grab the computer's mouse, but Tess snatched it away from him, slapping his hand back.

"Hands off. As you'll remember, this is my company's computer and you're not allowed to touch it."

"That's such shit and you know it," Gabe seethed, continuing to pace.

"How could you, Gabe? Honestly? After everything I've done for you? You knew this was the one thing I'd never get over. You knew how important trust was to me – you *knew*. This is the way you treat me?" Tess searched his face, looking for any sign of remorse.

"It's just… I don't know. I screwed up. She was just there, and a distraction from everything, I guess." Gabe stopped to lean across the desk to Tess. "I swear to you, she means nothing. I love *you*, Tess, not her."

Tess wasn't buying it.

"I should've expected this, honestly, I really should

have. It's not like you've been particularly trustworthy in the past, but I thought we'd moved past all that. I had hoped I wouldn't be another one of your casualties, and that you'd learn to love yourself enough to not do this to the person you're with, like so many times before." Tess crossed her arms as she leveled a glare at Gabe. "I guess I thought I'd be enough for you, Gabe. That I'd be the one to change you. My mistake."

"You are, Tess, I swear you are. You're more than enough for me. I don't deserve you." Gabe held his hands out to her. "Please, we can work through this."

Tess shook her head, ice flowing through her veins.

"You're right, Gabe. You don't deserve me."

He smiled. "Look, babe, you are making way too big a deal –"

She cut him off. "I've moved all the money and changed the passwords on all the accounts." She met his eyes dead-on. "Pack a bag and get out."

He stared at her, breathing through his nose, his chest rising and falling rapidly, rage clouding a face she'd once thought to be handsome.

"You don't have to be such a bitch about it," Gabe said coldly. Then he smirked. There it was – just a glimmer of joy in taking his power back.

Tess was a contrary sort, however. And now seemed like the perfect time to stop listening to what people – most notably, Gabe – told her to do.

Bitch, she thought. Yeah, she could get behind that.

Available as an e-book, Hardback, Paperback, Audio or Large Print.

Read Today

"**Ms. Bitch is sunshine in a book! An uplifting story of fighting your way through heartbreak and making your own version of happily-ever-after.**"
~Ann Charles, USA Today Bestselling Author of the Deadwood Mystery Series

"**Authentic and relatable, Ms. Bitch packs an emotional punch. By the end, I was crying happy tears and ready to pack my bags in search of my best life.**"
-Annabel Chase, author of the Starry Hollow Witches series

"**It's easy to be brave when you have a lot of support in your life, but it takes a special kind of courage to forge a new path when you're alone. Tess is the heroine I hope I'll be if my life ever crumbles down around me. Ms. Bitch is a journey of determination, a study in self-love, and a hope for second chances. I could not put it down!**"
-Renee George, USA Today Bestselling Author of the Nora Black Midlife Psychic Mysteries

"**I don't know where to start listing all the reasons why you should read this book. It's empowering. It's fierce. It's about loving yourself enough to build the life you want. It was honest, and raw, and real and I just...loved it so much!**"
– Sara Wylde, author of Fat

Available Now

THE ISLE OF DESTINY SERIES

ALSO BY TRICIA O'MALLEY

Stone Song

Sword Song

Spear Song

Sphere Song

"Love this series. I will read this multiple times. Keeps you on the edge of your seat. It has action, excitement and romance all in one series."- Amazon Review

Available in audio, e-book & paperback!

Available Now

"I have read thousands of books and a fair percentage have been romances. Until I read Wild Irish Heart, I never had a book actually make me believe in love."- Amazon Review

Available in audio, e-book & paperback!

Available Now

THE SIREN ISLAND SERIES

ALSO BY TRICIA O'MALLEY

Good Girl

Up to No Good

A Good Chance

Good Moon Rising

Too Good to Be True

A Good Soul

"Love her books and was excited for a totally new and different one! Once again, she did NOT disappoint! Magical in multiple ways and on multiple levels. Her writing style, while similar to that of Nora Roberts, kicks it up a notch!! I want to visit that island, stay in the B&B and meet the gals who run it! The characters are THAT real!!!" - Amazon Review

Available in audio, e-book & paperback!

Available Now

THE ALTHEA ROSE SERIES

ALSO BY TRICIA O'MALLEY

One Tequila

Tequila for Two

Tequila Will Kill Ya (Novella)

Three Tequilas

Tequila Shots & Valentine Knots (Novella)

Tequila Four

A Fifth of Tequila

A Sixer of Tequila

Seven Deadly Tequilas

Eight Ways to Tequila

"Not my usual genre but couldn't resist the Florida Keys setting. I was hooked from the first page. A fun read with just the right amount of crazy! Will definitely follow this series."- Amazon Review

Available in audio, e-book & paperback!

Available Now

AUTHOR'S NOTE

Ireland holds a special place in my heart – a land of dreamers and for dreamers. There's nothing quite like cozying up next to a fire in a pub and listening to a session or having a cup of tea while the rain mists outside the window. I'll forever be enchanted by her rocky shores and I hope you enjoy this series as much as I enjoyed writing it. Thank you for taking part in my world, I hope that my stories bring you great joy.

Have you read books from my other series? Join our little community by signing up for my newsletter for updates on island-living, fun giveaways, and how to follow me on social media!
http://eepurl.com/1LAiz.

or at my website
www.triciaomalley.com

Please consider leaving a review! Your review helps others to take a chance on my stories. I really appreciate your help!

AUTHOR'S ACKNOWLEDGEMENT

First, and foremost, I'd like to thank my family and friends for their constant support, advice, and ideas. You've all proven to make a difference on my path. And, to my beta readers, I love you for all of your support and fascinating feedback!

And last, but never least, my two constant companions as I struggle through words on my computer each day - Briggs and Blue.

Made in United States
Orlando, FL
27 December 2023

41687926R00171